THE MOON PIRATES

By
NEIL R. JONES

Illustrated by
Leo Morey

I0616709

ARMCHAIR FICTION
PO Box 4369, Medford, Oregon 97504

BLOODLUST DEEP UNDER THE MOON'S SURFACE...

Neil R. Jones' "The Moon Pirates" is an extraordinary science fiction adventure tale. The plot is simple: A group of space liner passengers is abducted by a band of space buccaneers and taken to a secret underground lair on the moon where they face unimaginable brutality from their bloodthirsty captors. No...you'll find no serious themes or underlying intellectual thought here. It's a straightforward piece of space opera, written in a style similar to Jones' wildly successful Professor Jameson tales. Yet this tale stands out for its sheer over-the-top depictions of violence and cruelty. These moon pirates are not nice people, inflicting unthinkable acts of barbarism against their captives. One of the main antagonists, Nez Hulan, is a character out of your worst nightmares—half-man, half machine, consisting of mechanical limbs, an aluminum-plated skull, metal ears, and a rubber heart. "The Moon Pirates" is an outer space roller coaster ride from start to finish.

FOR A COMPLETE SECOND NOVEL, TURN TO PAGE 119

CAST OF CHARACTERS

JAN TRENTON

Having survived a space disaster, this tough veteran astronaut was considered as fearless as they came; but his ship coming under siege by moon pirates put his courage to the ultimate test.

NEZ HULAN

Madder than the maddest mad scientist, this inhuman beast was more machine than man. His perverted intellect held deep hatred for all things decent; abject cruelty was his favorite hobby.

SUZETTE CLARKSFORD

She was beautiful and full of typical female frailties, yet strong enough to mentally withstand the atrocities of homicidal space pirate thugs. She also held the key to Jay Trenton's heart.

CARCONTE

This loutish maniac held total control over a savage band of outer space buccaneers through his craftiness, ruthlessness, and unyielding sense of pure barbarism.

JAMES CLARKSFORD

He was an extraordinarily successful interplanetary businessman on his way to Mars; but this latest venture into space turned out to be a real heads-up experience for him.

BALFOUR

One of only five passengers on the Interplanetary Limited, he was thought to be traveling to Mars to study Martian rain machines—but what was his real motive?

CHAPTER ONE
Aboard the Interplanetary Flyer

JAMES C. CLARKFORD, wealthy, manufacturer of middle-age, snapped off the television screen in the back of the seat ahead of him, removed the metal sound-cap from off his head and settled back comfortably against the upholstered cushions of the interplanetary liner that was coursing upon its regular, prescribed route to Venus. Clarkford and his daughter had boarded the interplanetary flyer that morning, and having been over the route many times before, he was becoming just a bit bored, wishing that something would happen to stir up excitement.

If Clarkford was bored, his daughter's attitude towards the trip was in extreme contrast to his own. With shapely form settled comfortably at full length upon a lounge, and with chin cupped in her hands, the girl gazed out of the thick, transparent windows into the depths of universal space. A wealth of wavy brown hair fell to her shoulders, while her blue, fathomless eyes were of that innocently penetrating nature that seeks out the very soul of a man in their searching quest. The oval of her pretty face was now directed towards the beauteous wonders of cosmic space, which lay spread before her.

Far off in the depths of the dark void, the galaxy of the Milky Way lay like a fiery band across the heavens, its myriad of stars lying scattered across the vast expanse of the sky like daisies in a long, winding, twisting lane. Although this was not the initial trip for Suzette Clarkford, she never lost interest in gazing spellbound at the wonderful display offered to the interplanetary traveler.

From where she watched, Suzette could see the planet Earth, dwindling away into millions of miles distance far behind them, its satellite, the moon, a point of light beside its huge contemporary. The sun was upon the other side of the spacecraft, and was therefore lost to the view of the occupants ranged by the opposite windows. Suzette looked at the dazzling orb of Venus, which they were rapidly approaching.

"Isn't it just beautiful, daddy?" exclaimed the girl.

"Yes, it certainly is," agreed her father. "But after you have ridden these interplanetary flyers as long as I have, they will offer no special interest to you, Sue."

"Oh, no!" remonstrated the girl. "I'll always love it. It's so wonderful—vast—mysterious—and weird! What fun it must be to pilot one of these!"

"WE are nearly there," said her father. "I hope that I find Dempster all right. I've come across thirty million miles of space to see him. Just before I left, I received two radio reports. The one from Mars stated that he had left a day or so ago on the interplanetary flight for Venus, while the information from Venus stated that the interplanetary ship was expected to arrive soon from Mars. It would seem, then, that Dempster is already there."

"Oh, your business, daddy!" deplored the girl as she came to sit by her father and embrace him. "Why don't you forget it sometimes—and not let it weigh you down so much."

The wealthy manufacturer smiled at his daughter's attempt to compel him to abandon his cares for a while.

"I'll forget it all until we get back to Earth after I've seen Dempster," said Clarkford. "This represents a big deal that includes projects on three planets. It is very important."

"Come up in the observatory," suggested the girl. "We shall be landing inside of half an hour, and I like to watch our descent from space, especially upon Venus. It's so wild, untamed and primitive—and beautiful. With its riot of

teeming life it's so vastly different from the sad, desolate surface of Mars. Come, daddy."

The girl skipped along through the huge space flyer, leading her father by the hand until they reached an elevator, which took them to the observatory in the top of the craft.

And while they prepared to view the descent of the space flyer upon the cloud covered expanse of Venus' surface, the interplanetary liner raced nearer the silver sphere at a tremendous speed that was only possible in a vacuum. It was the year 2564 A.D. Man had conquered the realms of space, even as he had previously conquered the air, and gigantic space liners now made regular trips among the three planets, Mars, Venus, and the Earth.

Following the first space flights to these planets, representing man's pioneer efforts at crossing the boundaries of space after a series of successive failures and disasters, it was found that on neither of these planets was there a race of intelligent beings. Both supported life—Mars' meager plant and animal life contrasting strangely with the luxuriant vegetation and teeming life amid the swamps and steaming jungles of the Venerian globe.

Mars, even though its atmosphere was of a rare, thin composition, was found habitable for certain individuals, and had been colonized from the Earth. Enough remained of aged relics and hieroglyphics upon the Martian world to assure geologists that on a far gone day in the dim past, a highly intelligent race, superior to man in intellectual attainments, had flourished upon the little red planet, but had for some reason met a wholesale extinction, or else had dwindled away through the passing of years, leaving after them a limited number of various lower types of animal life and a sparse scattering of plant life. The environment of the Martian globe had been such that with the scientific resources of the Earth it had been made habitable for mankind, being colonized along with Venus, to relieve the Earth's serious population problem.

THE conditions upon Venus were found to be radically different, and at first it had been a continual fight for existence with the fierce creatures and colossal monstrosities that inhabited the Venetian world.

The room in which Suzette Clarkford and her father found themselves was the observatory, a superstructure upon the oblong spaceship. The two were not alone; there were fully a dozen others within the lookout chamber, and all eyes were centered upon the huge globe below them encased in its feathery, shining cloud mass.

As the spaceship neared the gravitational attraction of the planet, its speed was reduced, and the flow of atomic energy was reversed somewhat to offset the mighty pull of the globe. It loomed closer and closer—until suddenly they were surrounded by a thick impenetrable fog of milky whiteness. For several moments they appeared to be suspended within this blanket of moisture particles, until finally they broke through. The space flyer from the Earth had pierced the cloud blanket of Venus, and was now cruising a mile or more above the surface. Stretching below them through the distance to the very rim of the horizon, as far as the eye could reach, a mass of yellow-hued vegetation grew to a great height.

The ship dropped lower as it cruised above the surface of Venus, and now those within the observatory of the interplanetary flyer could view the more minute details of the planet.

Gigantic forms lumbered, ungainly through the yellow forests, raising their huge snouts to bellow defiance at the spaceship.

"Oh, look, daddy!" exclaimed Sue suddenly. "Down there!" the girl pointed her finger at a small clearing in the forest of yellow, swaying branches.

"Is it a battle of monsters?" exclaimed Clarkford.

Below them in the forest, two nightmarish engines of flesh and blood were preparing to tear one another asunder with the mighty weapons that nature had bestowed upon them! One of the creatures was formed like a great snake with a long body some five feet in diameter, having a series of some eight or ten sets of long legs that held it above the ground. The great, glittering rows of teeth that lined the terrible jaws of the animal were outstretched to a span of some twelve feet, ready to close upon the anatomy of its equally fearsome adversary at the first opportunity. Its opponent was just as large, though of a more compact build, being of towering proportions mounted on three sets of legs. From all sides huge, curling tentacles waved nervously as the other beast approached. Four little eyes gleamed wickedly from the squat, diminutive head that, devoid of any neck, sprouted from the upper forepart of the creature's colossal bulk. The tail of the animal curled and switched as it stood, waiting defensively for the charge of the other snakelike creature. The latter, its wide jaws distended, was rushing forward madly.

"What terrible things!" breathed the girl excitedly as she viewed the grotesque creations that roamed the forests of Venus.

AND now there broke forth upon the ears of the spaceship passengers the most terrifying, blood-curdling roars, howls, mouthings, and screams they had ever heard, the radio phones upon the outside of the craft conducting the sounds of conflict to the ears of those within.

The first animal leaped forward and seized a goodly portion of the second creature within its wide jaws, which closed tightly in a vise-like grip! The bulky animal writhed and roared in the terrible grasp of the attacker. As its powerful tentacles closed upon the long, twisting body of the other in a death hold, a large section of the animal was torn loose. And now the witnesses to the primitive, mortal combat saw the effects of the tightening tentacles upon the body of the wide jawed animal. The edges of the tentacles were lined with razor-edged segment; and as the tentacles closed tightly, working back and forth in a rapid motion, the body of the attacking beast was cleaved into three or four sections, which continued to wriggle and twist separately in their death throes! The head of the disgusting creature released its mouthful of living flesh and seized upon the huge animal in a new spot!

The second beast, with victory within his grasp, though bleeding to death, stiffened spasmodically at this second onslaught, while the great jaws crunched together for the last time and froze, the bodily remains of the animal still squirming, the long legs kicking!

"How terrible!" shuddered the girl as she shrank back from the grisly sight.

As if by prearranged signal, there broke forth from the surrounding forest below a pack of animals as large as horses, running swiftly forward on ten legs, they appeared to be a cross between an animal and insect, for a series of antennae arose from their beads, while the covering on their backs was such as one sees on beetles. Their jaws were those of an animal, and from between them there issued dismal howls as the dozen or more of these denizens of the yellow forest broke forth into the clearing from the surrounding verdure. They had been impatiently awaiting the outcome of the conflict between the forest giants. They leaped, fought and howled, their weird cries wailing in concert as they viciously attacked and devoured the remains of the two great beasts that had fought and died within the short space of a few minutes.

"This is a repetition of what took place when our own world was young—during the Mesozoic age," said Clarkford to the girl. "Though of course there were different types of animals and trees than we see here."

AS the flyer reached a certain level over this flatland surface of the planet, it put on more speed so that the terrain now swung dizzily past them in one continuous blotch of yellow. Several times, huge shadowy forms flitted about them on wings, rising up to meet them, or descending from a higher altitude. The speed of the ship was so great that they were always left in the rear.

"Flying reptiles," explained the business man to his daughter, "or what are technically known as pterodactyls. They are fearless, of an extremely combative nature, and are continually attacking the smaller space flyers on Venus."

"There's the city!" cried the girl pointing far off on the horizon above the forest where a high globe arose like a bubble. "We are nearly there!"

"Yes—it's Deliphon, the first stop of the spaceship," said Clarkford.

Rapidly the ship approached the Venerian city, which was protected from the frequent rains and terrible storms, as well as from the huge swarms of insects and lumbering giants of the forest, by a transparent dome that covered the entire city from end to end. As the space liner soared above the enclosed metropolis, the tall buildings could be seen through their transparent covering, rising to meet the city ceiling.

In the center of the dome, a series of openings appeared to give the space flyer from Earth an entrance. The interplanetary liner lowered itself through into the city, beneath the high dome, cruising very slowly through the maze of air traffic to a broad central building, which towered above all others within the city.

The massive structures arose to over one hundred stories; the last five floors comprising open air landing bases for aircraft and space flyers. The interplanetary liner headed for the fourth level, or the one just under the roof. Under the expert management of its pilot, the giant of the skies came safely to rest upon the fourth level.

"Well, we have arrived," remarked Clarkford.

"It was such an enjoyable trip!" exclaimed Suzette.

"Come," said her father as he hurried the girl to an elevator. This brought them from the fourth to the first of the five open air-levels where the city aircraft were located. Clarkford hired a small plane, and the two were taxied across the city to an office building, and soon he was in conference with members of the firm he had come to see.

AS he emerged from the offices to the ante-room in which his daughter awaited him, the latter noticed the worried look upon his face.

"What's the trouble, daddy?" queried the girl.

"Dempster—he isn't here."

"But didn't he come?"

"Yes, and then returned to Mars only a few hours after he had arrived."

"Didn't he know you were coming?"

"Evidently not. That's where I made my mistake. I should have sent a radio message to the interplanetary ship he was on, getting into direct communication with him, instead of talking with the station here at Venus and the one at Mars."

"What shall we do?" asked the girl, wide-eyed. "You've made the trip for nothing it seems—but, we can turn it into a pleasure trip."

"We must leave for Mars on the next interplanetary flight," stated the man with serious mien. "The next one leaves within six hours. With the present positions of Mars and Venus on their orbits, the trip will take approximately two and a half days."

"Why, there's nothing in that to be so discouraged about. It's a very good way in which to spend your vacation."

"The trouble is this—something I haven't told you about before," said the girl's father. "I have in my pockets bonds and papers worth over twenty million dollars, which I must personally turn over to Dempster or to one of the Martian officials of our business. I'll not be satisfied or free from concern until those bonds are off my hands and I can dismiss the matter from my mind."

"Oh…" exclaimed the girl. "Then of course you must see this man as soon as possible."

As the two conversed, they failed to notice a sallow-faced individual leaning against the wall a short distance from them to their rear taking in their conversation. Having heard the main part of their talk, he moved away from them unobserved.

"We must eat, make a change of clothing, and be ready to take the next spaceship to Mars," said Clarkford as the two retired to a dining hall.

CHAPTER TWO
Buccaneers of Space

WE shall now turn our attention to that cold, dead, desolated surface of the Earth's satellite, the moon, which represented a forlorn vista of melancholy loneliness. In all directions off in the boundless realms of interstellar space the fiery points of star light scintillated, and glittered from suns situated interminable eons of light years from this comparative speck of cosmic dust, the moon.

Between the pitted rim of a deep crater and a towering peak of rough, lunar rock, a lonely traveler picked his way through the barren valley of silence to the summit of the peak, accomplishing the ascent in enormous jumps, which he appeared to take with surprising ease of motion. The solitary scaler of this lunar peak was clad in a queer accoutrement of metal and an elastic substance to protect him from the frigidness of the low temperature, as well as from the burning, destroying rays of the sun. From spiked shoes to chest, the moon traveler's suit was composed in part of thick rubbery, material that yielded to his every motion. His chest, back and shoulders were encased in a sheeting of heavy, yellow metal, his arms being enclosed in the elastic material that terminated at the finger tips in steel claws, four claws on each hand, opening and closing at the will of the wearer. The head of the moon traveler was encased in a massive helmet, the front of which was of a transparent substance, through which the man peered as he made his way over the dismal surface of the dead satellite.

Having gained the lunar rise, the man turned and looked backward down the slope of rough, jagged rock formations he had just traversed. Raising his eyes, he looked miles away into the distance where outlined vividly in the airless void surrounding the moon, each detail of the lunar topography was as clearly portrayed to his view as if it were no farther than a distance of twenty feet from him. On all sides lay the towering hills stretching away to meet the rough surfaced mountains which loomed still further skyward. Stars gleamed in riotous profusion against the background of intense blackness.

He continued on once more, taking a leap, which carried him a distance of fully twenty feet across a deep gash to a small plateau. From this he essayed another jump to the semi-flat surface of another rise across a low depression of uneven surface. His calculations fell short of the described destination. The leap had left him a foot or two short of his prospective landing place, his feet striking the side of the rugged outcrop of rock and sliding downward toward the abyss that yawned beneath him. Frantically the claws on the arm-extremities of the suit opened and closed rapidly as the moon traveler attempted to gain a hold upon the rough side of the peak down which he slid toward the unknown depths of the black pit below him. A landslide of fine particles and larger pieces of moon rock accompanied him, but there was no rising of dust such as would have happened had there been an atmosphere.

Finally the spiked feet of the man caught upon an outcropping of rock that did not give way beneath him and his swift descent was terminated. From here, he gave a leap that carried him to the summit some twenty feet over his head, and then, in long, fantastic leaps, he continued his journey across the irregular surface of the moon until he arrived upon the rim of a crater. The sides stretched away into the distance, the diameter of the crater hole being fully three miles across from rim to rim. Looking into its depth, the moon traveler surveyed the sloping sides of the pit that extended downward into the gloom.

HE walked along the edge of the crater for a short distance until he reached a certain point on the crater's lip where the interior of the gigantic, circular depression dropped vertically towards the bottom of the broad crater hole.

The ring of an iron ladder was set in the lip of the crater wall, and extending downward were a succession of more ladder rungs. Down these the moon traveler climbed, disappearing into the blackness, being suddenly lost to view from the sunlight as he continued his descent into the crater. Reaching a depth of some three hundred feet below the crater's rim, the man stepped off of the ladder upon a small platform set in the wall of the pit. Before him lay a tunnel's mouth and into this he walked, the absolute gloom of the pit being supplanted by an ethereal glow, which appeared to emanate from the walls of the tunnel, exuding a soft, dim brilliance. The moon traveler traversed the tunnel for a considerable distance until he emerged into a cavern of proportions slightly larger than the tunnel he had come through, and now before him stood an elevator such as might be found in any of the modern twenty-sixth century buildings.

The elevator car, like all of those at this period, was propelled by an explosion and rejection of atomic energy, and as the man entered and turned a lever slightly, the car shot rapidly downward, nor did it slacken its mad pace for the next mile's descent, until it stopped. The moon traveler left the car, walked through a short tunnel to where a portion of the rock slid aside to allow him entrance to a small chamber. The rock wall then slid noiselessly back into place after he had entered.

He pressed several large, metal knobs set in the wall, and a hissing of air sounded as the semi-vacuum of the airlock chamber was filled with the respiratory atmosphere of nitrogen and oxygen. He now turned his attention to a long rack at one side of the room where there hung an array of suits and helmets similar to the one which he wore. The moon traveler removed his helmet first of all, and then, unlocked the air rejuvenator from his back after which he emerged from the rest of his moon-surface suit, hanging it carefully alongside the others.

A buzz of voices became noticeable as the man strode along the tunnel towards an open doorway at the far end. The voices became louder and more garrulous as he neared the entrance. As he came in, a voice greeted him.

"Hello, Bender, we have some very good news for you— news which our remarkable Zind has just radioed to us from the Deliphon city at Venus!"

THE underground chamber was a luxuriously furnished room, which would have done credit to the wealthiest homes on any of the three planets, had it not been so garishly outfitted and overdone with a lack of taste for harmony. Certainly the furnishings of the place were of the finest and most expensive, but their arrangement and contrast were like the assortment of ruffians and ill natured crew that lounged comfortably within this hidden lunar cavern. Fully a dozen men either reclined at ease within the long room or else were engaged in some trivial occupation to while away the time. From this great central chamber, doorways led in all directions, and from the various sounds that came out of them it was evident that these dozen or so men did not constitute the entire group that occupied the subterranean chambers of the moon.

The squint-eyed little man who had addressed Bender now continued.

"It's more rich hauls for us, comrade, the richest we have ever laid hands upon yet."

"Is that so, Terseg?" queried Bender.

"Yes, very much so—we are going to capture the *Interplanetary Limited* between Venus and Mars. It contains shipments of gold and valuable merchandise—and that isn't all, so Zind tells us. A passenger upon it carries a fortune in bonds with him…"

"But that's too dangerous!" expostulated Bender, addressing the men as a group. "We haven't the fighting equipment to overcome a large ship such as that—and if we should succeed, we'd bring the wrath and destruction of the three worlds down about our heads! It is safer to stick to the smaller private interplanetary ships. We can make a good living out of plundering the smaller merchant craft that fly among the three planets."

"Well, that's what I think, too," agreed the Terseg. He had derived his name from the fact that his squint eyes and queer shaped, peaked nose gave him the expression of the Terseg bird, which was one of the commoner species of Martian ornithology.

"SILENCE!" thundered a squat-built, dark-visaged man with a bald head.

"Is this mutiny? I'm the leader here—and whoever contests the fad gets the disintegrator gun or the ejector tube! You're not to do any thinking, Terseg—Hulan and I do that! I lead the crowd, and make our plans—Hulan carries out all of the scientific details. If I hear any more opposition from you, Bender, it's the disintegrator gun for you—or maybe Hulan will have a more unique idea, eh, Hulan?"

A cruel, thin-lipped smile was the only answer from the man across the table from Carconte, the pirate leader. It was a reply freighted with more significance than words could ever have carried. Though not as villainous appearing as his pirate chief, there was something about Hulan that made men shudder and fear him more than they did the verbose, terrifying Carconte. Perhaps it was because Hulan was half-machine and half-man.

Fully fifteen years before, Hulan, a scientific prodigy of the Martian university at Fomar, had been in an interplanetary wreck upon an expedition to the asteroid group adjacent to the mighty planet Jupiter. The meteor repelling rays of the space flyer had become impaired through some failure of the intricate mechanism to function perfectly. Tearing through the seas of space between worlds at a terrific speed, a huge meteor had smashed into the space flyer, reducing the interplanetary ship to a mass of junk, and killing its six occupants, including Hulan, outright.

The mass of wreckage and dead men became a satellite of Ceres for a period of three Earthly years before the remains of the spaceship with its grisly crew were recovered by a Venerian expedition to Jupiter and the asteroid group. The remains were towed to a Martian city. Here it was found that five of the dead spaceship crew were so torn and mangled as to be unrecognizable.

All six of the bodies were as perfectly preserved by the cold, germless vacuum of space, as they had been at the moment sudden death had stricken them from out of space. Hulan's body was the least marred of the six. Some of them had been decapitated and torn to shreds by the awful crash and rending of the meteoric impact, when the space wanderer had torn out of the cosmic void at the rate of fifteen miles per second. Hulan's arms and legs had been either torn to pieces or else were so mangled that the surgeons at the Martian hospital had found it necessary to amputate them. His skull had also been fractured in several places and, a piece of metal had punctured his heart.

Then followed the greatest surgical-mechanical feat any of the three worlds had ever known! Hulan's heart was taken out, a rubber one substituted; the upper section of his fractured cranium removed, and his brain replaced in a new aluminum skull; and he was brought back to life. For a year he had lain in an unconscious state while his wounded arm and leg stumps healed.

When they were sufficiently cured, Hulan was brought out of his coma of suspended animation and was equipped with mechanical arms and legs. The man who had been dead for three long years had been miraculously recalled to life. He now had a rubber heart, an aluminum brain pan, metal radiophone ears and mechanical arms and legs. Nez Hulan was truly a human robot.

THE results of the removal and replacement of his brain had stimulated the mentality of the man to such a degree that he was endowed with a greater intellect than had been the case before the accident. Sad to say, however, the super-intellect of his mind had been perverted to an evil, murderous morale, and the complicated, scientific deaths of several notables upon the Martian planet were finally traced to him. He had been forced to flee from Mars and keep under cover from interplanetary police and detectives. Finally he had joined the forces of the moon pirates, seeking protection and companionship in return for his devilish ingenuity.

And so the cruel smile of Hulan was more to be feared than the ominous, blood-curling threats of Carconte.

"Why—I—I merely suggested that it might be dangerous to the good of all," faltered Bender discreetly.

"He meant no harm, Carconte," said Hulan placatingly, his dull, monotonous voice breaking in upon the conversation for the first time. "He is just naturally cautious. If we find traitors or deserters in our ranks, well—"

Hulan raised his arm forward at full length; the light glistening on the bright metal limb, the strong steel fingers closing together in a significant clutch, as a wicked smile spread upon the face of the machine man. His features reflected the intellectual superiority he exercised above this motley crowd of scoundrels. Hulan's words were few, and, at what times he spoke, the rare occasion of his speeches lent particular emphasis to his words. He never failed to capture the attention of his listeners, for the man never dropped an idle word—they were always laden with deep import.

And so it was that every moon pirate in the room gazed silently at Hulan's gesturing, mechanical arm, and at the bald, aluminum pate with its pair of metal ears, the grotesque appearance of the man holding them spellbound for a moment.

"Terseg was right about those bonds," said Carconte. "Zind overheard some bankers in Deliphon say that this man was taking the *Interplanetary Limited* for Mars with twenty million dollars worth of bonds upon his person. Incidentally, Hulan and I have been planning for a long time to seize one of the interplanetary flights between Mars and Venus. They carry valuable consignments of gold and merchandise and the knowledge that this man with the bonds is to be aboard this particular flyer, is an added inducement for us to capture it."

"When do we start?" asked Bender, curiously.

"Tomorrow at noon," replied Carconte. "It's rich awards for all of us—another derelict spaceship destroyed and sent upon an endless journey out of the solar system—then back here to the rendezvous to plan a new venture. We'll have treasure, gold, and merchandise!"

"And maybe women!" added a grizzled old veteran of many a combat, his hideously scarred visage set in gloating anticipation.

"No women!" snapped Hulan's metallic voice, cryptically. "They bring disaster and death to such as we—they are a trouble and ruination to the best laid plans…"

"YOU and your damned rubber heart!" retaliated Scar Face. "You haven't the feelings of a human being. Just because you don't want a thing, the rest of us must forego it! We are not all hunks of iron and rubber, are we, friends?"

"Stop this infernal bickering!" roared Carconte. "I'll have the say as to whether we'll take women or not! If there are any on board the *Limited*, I'm the one to decide as to whether we shoot them out the ejector tube, or save them for the sport of the men—or for Hulan's laboratory! Now is no time to discuss the question, and when it's settled, no contraption of flesh and junk is going to decide—or any crowd of lily-livered poltroons either; I'm the supreme authority here! Get that? And now we'll lay our plans—sound the signal bell, and bring every man into the chamber…"

One of the men at the table leaned forward and depressed a button. A moment more and pirates came pouring into the central chamber from the adjoining rooms and corridors where they had been engaged in various occupations. They continued to fill up the broad room beneath the surface of the moon until over fifty of them were present. In here, there was none of the high jumping or awkward movements that had characterized the progress of Bender as he had wandered across the moon's surface just before his descent to the hangout of the moon pirates. The floors of these subterranean chambers of the Earth's satellite were composed of the same substance as that which made up the flooring of the spaceships, possessing a gravity attraction equal to that of Earth.

"All right, men!" shouted Carconte, standing upon the table where he could be seen by all his murderous crew; the desperate characters and outcasts of three worlds. "You probably know that tomorrow we embark on a new, hazardous venture, an escapade that is fraught with danger, something we have previously considered beyond our capabilities, but tomorrow we are going to capture the *Interplanetary Limited* between Venus and Mars!"

A roar of approval greeted these words, and then Carconte continued his outline of their plans.

"Before this, when considering the capture of these larger spaceships we have had to pass them up and confine our attentions to the smaller craft, so that we would not bring to the attention of Mars, Venus, and Earth the fact that an organization such as ours exists, but now Hulan feels that we can overcome these interplanetary giants, and the peoples of the three worlds will never know what became of the *Interplanetary Limited*, whose fate shall always remain a mystery.

"After the conquest of the *Limited*, and the pilfering and destruction of the craft with its passengers, we shall return here with the treasure, and then we can hide—up until the trouble blows over. It will be popular opinion that the ship was wrecked by a meteor and sent shooting off into space beyond the solar system."

The men were awed to silence by the magnitude of the idea their pirate chief had described to them. That the plan appealed to their venturesome spirits was indisputable, and so finally when the full import of the idea had sunk into their brains, they all joined in a rousing cheer, for their chief, and for the ingenuity of the scientific arch-fiend, Hulan, the human robot, whose perverted, super-intellect had made possible the many victories they had amassed to their credit.

"Overhaul the *Jolly Roger*, our interplanetary ship, and fit it up for our departure tomorrow!" shouted Carconte in his parting instructions before he jumped off the table and sent the men scurrying to their various duties. "Hulan has some new mechanical contrivances to be installed within the ship."

CHAPTER THREE
The Jolly Roger

UPON the interplanetary flight to Mars, Clarkford and his daughter rose from a refreshing breakfast following a pleasant night's rest aboard the spaceship, which had put many miles between its present position and the planet Venus. When referring to a night's rest in the depth of space where there is no night or day, but rather a paradoxical combination of both—the daylight sun shining from out of the star-studded darkness—the reference to a night's rest is conceived through the fact that Clarkford and his daughter were continuing their daily routine upon the basis of the Earth-time until they reached Mars.

And now they emerged into the luxurious parlor chamber of the *Interplanetary Limited,* which sped upon its way at a fantastic speed, covering several millions of miles every hour. Taking seats where they could look from the windows of the huge space flyer, the two talked over the situation.

We certainly had trouble getting aboard this flight," said the man. "They didn't seem to want to carry passengers."

"I wonder why?" queried Suzette. "There were plenty of passengers on the flyer we took to Venus, and here I don't believe that there are over three passengers besides us. Of course there is the crew, which numbers some eight individuals."

"Well, Sue," replied Clarkford, "you see this wasn't exactly a 'passenger' limited, but an 'express' limited, and it was strict orders for the astronauts to take on but few passengers, and these only under the strict recommendations of the Venerian government, and we surely had a hard time getting those in time to board this flight. If we hadn't received the papers just as we did it would have meant another delay of two days."

"But why are they so reticent about allowing us to ride?" asked the girl perplexed at the mysterious attitude the commander of the spaceship had taken in regards to their passage.

"Because they have a shipment of five hundred million dollars in gold, platinum and diamonds aboard," answered Clarkford.

THE girl gasped for breath, her eyes going wide at the mention of the vast sum.

"A half-billion…" she echoed faintly.

"Yes," replied her father, "and with so many crooks running loose now, they can be none too careful as to whom they take aboard, even though the valuables are under massive locks in strong vaults."

"And so their passenger list is limited to five—three people besides us," observed the girl.

"Yes. There is Mr. Balfour, the slim, dark-faced individual who's traveling to Mars to study the rain machines. Then there's Bert Sorelle who's joining a Martian expedition to Saturn to study the planet's rings, and then last of all we have Professor E. J. Crayton, who's a professor of botany at the Formar University, and who's returning to Mars after having passed several weeks upon Venus studying the Venerian flora."

"From what little I have seen of them, I believe I like Mr. Sorelle the best. He's so interesting and entertaining," remarked the girl.

"Yes," agreed Clarkford, "because he's an adventurer who has been at the most prominent places of action on three worlds, not to mention the numerous expeditions into space he has accompanied."

"Here he comes, now," whispered the girl.

A pleasant faced individual of middle age, in whose eye there still lurked the spirit of carefree, adventurous youth, walked towards them from the entrance to the dining saloon.

"Good evening," he greeted them cheerily.

"Good evening?" queried the girl. "You mean 'Good morning,' My father and I just came from the breakfast table."

"And I from my supper," laughed Sorelle. "I see where I must change my sleeping hours, if I'm to see much of you folks during this trip. I assume you are on Earth time; well, I'm on Martian time, the eastern hemisphere time, which at the present brings your night and my day in conjunction. I must change over, or I'm going to be deuced lonesome. There are only four passengers besides myself, and they all seem to be eating and sleeping on a different time schedule than mine."

Clarkford laughed heartily at the ludicrous situation.

"What do you say we all take a trip up into the observatory and watch the Earth as we spin past it?" he suggested.

"Oh, fine!" said Suzette, clapping her hands together.

"Suits me," agreed Bret Sorelle.

The three started for the superstructural chamber of the observatory whose transparent walls would allow them a glimpse of the cosmic skies.

"Pardon me," spoke a handsome, dark-faced man whose thin willowy figure bent in a polite, apologetic gesture, "but you wouldn't mind if I accompanied you?"

"Certainly not, Mr. Balfour," replied Clarkford to the individual who had just entered the parlor. "We shall be glad to have you with us."

"Thank you, sir," and the scientist, who was traveling to Mars in connection with an interest in the rain machines of that cloudless planet, brought the number of the group to four.

THEY entered the observatory to find Professor Crayton talking with a member of the crew, whose uniform proclaimed him to be one of the two pilots who alternated with each other in the management of the space flyer. Professor Crayton was speaking.

"Yes. Trenton, it is true that the flowering shrubs of Venus owe their excessive size to the fact that the atmosphere is so humid."

At the mention of the man's name as the four entered the room, Clarkford sprang forward.

"Is your name Jan Trenton? Jan Trenton—the astronaut who had the encounter with the death's head meteor?"

"Yes sir, that's who I am," admitted the young man, "but I can assure you that we'll have no encounter with meteors this trip, for our repellor rays steer us off their course."

"Oh, I have no fear on that score," laughed Clarkford, gripping the hand of the young astronaut in a hearty shake. "I heard of your exploit right after it had happened six months ago. A radio news dispatch from Mars gave us a firsthand description of it following your return to that planet when your space flyer tore loose from the meteor in the upper reaches of the Martian atmosphere. You folks all remember that, don't you?"

"I remember, daddy," said the girl gazing in open admiration at the young pilot of the *Interplanetary Limited*. "His picture was broadcast over the television units."

"And thrilled the world with an account of your unique adventure, Mr. Trenton," added Bret Sorelle, the adventurer. "I've been all over the three worlds and three moons, and in my time I have enjoyed quite a number of harrowing, death-defying adventures and thrills, but in all my career I profess I haven't had one which matches that of the death's head meteor."

"I was a witness to part of the tragedy, or rather near tragedy," announced Professor Crayton. "I was within thirty miles of where the meteor struck. I saw the flaming body tear down out of the atmosphere, and heard the terrible concussion as it landed."

"They dug the meteor out of the ground," observed Balfour, "and now what's left of it is on exhibition at the museum in Mendex. I saw it there the last time I was in the Martian city."

"Yes," replied Professor Crayton, "but what is on view at Mendex isn't one-twentieth part of the original meteor. It's merely the burnt out fragment of one of the pieces after the explosion."

"What ever happened," asked the girl, "that made your spaceship break away from the meteor just in time? Why didn't it break away sooner?"

"Well, you see it was like this," explained the astronaut. "If you remember, I left the drill and release of atomic energy running at full speed. The terrific release of atomic energy coming in contact with the solidity of the atmosphere acted the same as a kick of dynamite, producing an immense inertia that blew my space car right off from the side of the meteor, breaking off the chunk of the meteor that had been loosened by the drilling. That small meteorite fragment that broke off and clung to my spaceship, when it was cast back into space, is now mounted on a pedestal in the astronaut's station at the Meteorological Bureau in Denver, Colorado."

"A cool head is what saved you, my lad," said Clarkford.

"It was the closest to death I've ever come," said Trenton.

"The closest anyone could expect to come without dying," observed Sorelle.

"DID you ever hear of the case of Nez Hulan?" queried Crayton.

"You mean the man who lay dead in space for three years, and was brought back to life again after having been given a new heart made of rubber and his fractured skull replaced by an aluminum brain case?" queried Clarkford.

"Yes," replied Sorelle. "Who hasn't heard of it—the most famous surgical operation in history. His arms and legs were found so torn and mangled, that their amputation was necessary. It seems that he was supplied with mechanical legs and arms as well as with metal radiophone ears built into his aluminum skull."

"Before the catastrophe among the asteroids, he was my pupil at Fomar," stated the professor.

"And since then he has been convicted of murder—escaped the authorities of three planets, and is either dead or else has gone into hiding," said Clarkford. "No one has heard of him for several years."

During the latter part of the conversation, Balfour remained strangely silent, apparently content to listen to the comments of the others concerning the mechanical-limbed man.

Trenton and Suzette Clarkford were no longer interested in the general trend of conversation, but were training one of the long, protruding telescopes of the observatory upon the distant planet they were passing by, largest of the three consecutive worlds, the Earth, which at that particular time was at distance of fifteen million miles from the route of the *Interplanetary Limited,* the closest they would come to the rotating sphere.

"There's the moon!" exclaimed the girl. "See…it's just peering over the rim of the Earth, on the other side of the planet."

"I never cared much for that place," remarked the jovial Sorelle who had joined the astronaut and daughter of the wealthy Mr. Clarkford. "There's something about it that always gives me the creeps—some intangible, depressing feeling which I cannot accurately describe. I never felt that way on either of the two moons of Mars."

"I've never been on the moon," said the girl. "My father has promised to take me there someday."

"I expect to see more moons than I'll be able to count, pretty soon," said Sorelle.

"How is that?" asked Trenton curiously.

"I'm on that Martian expedition to Saturn to study the small moonlets that compromise its rings," replied Sorelle.

"That will be interesting," said Trenton. "I have never been any farther than Jupiter. I was on a trip once, through the asteroids."

A member of the crew now came in and spoke a few words to Jan Trenton, who in turn addressed the girl.

"I must leave now to take over the control of the ship. Brentley's spell is ended for the time being. I hope to see you again before the trip's over."

Bidding the little group goodbye, the astronaut left to assume control of the *Interplanetary Limited*, while the five sole passengers of the space liner continued their viewing of the Earth, moon, planets and stars, the latter twinkling brilliantly in scattered profusion.

IN the pilot's control room of the *Interplanetary Limited*, Jan Trenton relieved Brentley, taking over the piloting of the huge spaceship through the infinite depths of the cosmic vacuum towards the red planet of Mars, the outermost of the three consecutive planets that bore life and civilization. The astronaut set the nose of the craft ahead of the red disc of light, which marked the fourth satellite of the sun's incandescent mass, and then settled back to ruminate upon the trip, and upon his comparatively new position as pilot of the *Interplanetary Limited*.

Following his encounter with the death's head meteor, he had won promotion from the ranks of the Meteorological Bureau's staff of astronauts to the coveted position of pilot of the *Interplanetary Limited* between Venus and Mars. This represented his fourth month in the service, and his capability and punctuality had already won him commendation.

He liked the position; it brought him into contact with a number of interesting and delightful people, and represented a direct contrast to the lonesome work in which he had been engaged while in the employ of the Meteorological Bureau. His thoughts reverted to the sweet face of the girl with the sparkling eyes who had stood with him a few moments before the telescope. How lovely she was, thought Jan, looking upon the far off planet of Mars whose red eye shone like a ruby amidst the scintillating sapphires and diamonds of star points. Never had he seen such bewitching eyes—nor such lustrous, wavy, brown hair, and she radiated such a charming personality.

He sighed, for among his thoughts there arose the realization of the gulf that lay between their stations in life. He let his eyes drop from the red planet to the control board.

AS his eyes fell upon the control board, he gasped in sudden astonishment! He had unconsciously diminished the speed of the space flyer to half of its cruising speed while engrossed in his reverie! Quickly, his hand shot forth to increase the release of atomic energy back to normal once more. It was already shoved back to its limit—but the dials only registered half speed! What was wrong? Hastily, he radioed the machine room—everything down there apparently functioned perfectly. Again he referred to his dial, and with a qualm of dismay and perplexity he saw that it registered less than half, and was rapidly dropping. What was happening? Surely there was no celestial object close enough to affect the speed of the space liner in such a strange manner.

A dial which recorded the presence of large meteors now caught the attention of the pilot as he saw the needle slowly swing around from its neutral position in the transparent sphere where it was suspended, and point directly to their rear, a bit downward. There could be no meteors of great size in the vicinity that would affect the speed of the spaceship to such an extent. One of the larger asteroids might have had such an effect as to curtail the speed of the space liner until it should have passed the vicinity of the little world's attraction, but the nearest asteroid was Eros, which careened like some colossal mountain through space upon its orbit beyond Mars. Again he looked at the dial—it had dropped still further, and as he watched he saw the needle move perceptibly to a lower rate of speed! The astronaut was aghast, and tested the mechanism of the dial. It was working perfectly.

Meanwhile, the passengers and crew of the *Interplanetary Limited* were unaware of the abating speed of the space liner. Movement in space is imperceptible, because in the immense vacuum there is nothing by which to make comparisons, and a space traveler may be progressing at the rate of several million miles an hour and be no more conscious of the fact than if he were moving at a very low rate of speed.

It was not until the spaceship had actually come to a stop that any of the passengers or crew became aware that something beyond the regular routine of interplanetary travel was taking place.

The five passengers had all left the observatory and were now assembled once more in the parlor.

"I feel that something's wrong!" remarked Suzette Clarkford, the furrows of a deep frown mantling her pretty brow. "Things don't seem just right…"

"Your imagination, my dear," admonished her father.

Sorelle and Balfour were engaged in gazing from the windows of the spacecraft. At the girl's words he turned from his position on the lounge and made the following remark:

"I feel that way, too. It's rather a premonition of evil, which I've experienced before."

"Really, I see no cause for alarm," spoke Balfour, a smile spreading upon his olive-tinted countenance. "A case of imagination, as Mr. Clarkford has suggested."

Professor Crayton was silent, being absorbed in a book, and completely oblivious of the conversation of his fellow passengers.

Presently, Brentley, the co-pilot working in alternation with Jan Trenton, came in with a troubled scowl across his face.

"DO you people know that this spaceship is at a comparative standstill, and that some mysterious force is holding us back?" asked Brentley. "The atomic discharges are still taking place, and by all present known laws of interstellar locomotion we should be speeding across space at several million miles per hour. Trenton is working at the controls, trying to get us out of this jam, but he says there isn't anything wrong with the ship; that there's an ulterior power that is holding us within its attraction. We thought it to be only fair for you people to know."

"I knew something was wrong!" exclaimed the girl, frightened by the mysterious force which had acted upon her subconsciousness, even before Brentley had made his startling announcement.

"What can it be?" said Clarkford in surprise.

Professor Crayton had dropped his book on hearing the words of Brentley, and now he viewed the situation with alarm and consternation.

"Most unusual!" he remarked.

Sorelle said nothing, but it was apparent that he was thinking rapidly, and now he turned his attentions to the windows of the space liner.

"Fear not, people," spoke the smooth voice of Balfour. "Our remarkable friend Mr. Trenton, will no doubt solve the problem, and we shall be safely upon our way once more."

Of the five passengers, Mr. Balfour appeared to be the least perturbed of the group, and he attempted to quell the fears and anxieties of the rest.

Suddenly a shout arose from Bret Sorelle who peered from the window out into the depths of space.

"Come here—everybody!" he yelled. "Out there is the thing, whatever it is, that is holding us back!"

There followed a grand rush to the window, and five sets of eyes were directed upon a huge, shadowy monster, which lurked in their rear and was slowly stealing alongside of them.

"What is it?" whispered Professor Crayton hoarsely.

"Another spaceship!" replied Sorelle.

"What is it doing here?" queried Clarkford.

"We'll probably soon find out," said Balfour suggestively.

The mysterious prowler of the dark realms of space swung alongside the *Interplanetary Limited* until a bare hundred feet separated the two. It was only half as large as the space liner.

From its sides there bristled several long spikes whose tips shone with a queer light, and from the prow of the craft a long tube projected.

"Look at that horrid emblem upon the front of the ship!" spoke the girl whose heart was pounding rapidly under the stress of excitement.

All eyes were now directed upon a white blotch of color against the sides of the black space wanderer where the sunlight reflected.

"A skull and bones!" exclaimed Professor Crayton.

"What does it mean?" asked Clarkford.

"Death!" said Bret Sorelle. "It's the skull and cross bones of free booters, the *Jolly Roger!* It can mean only one thing—pirates!"

CHAPTER FOUR
Captivity

Up out of the moon crater, the pirate ship, under the skilled control of Hulan, with Carconte, at his side, soared above the dead, lonely surface of the Earth's satellite into the immensities of solar space, leaving the fixed globe of the lunar satellite far behind. Hulan directed the *Jolly Roger* away from the satellite and its parent body, which lay some quarter of a million miles off into space. Within the spaceship were some twenty-five of the moon pirates who had been picked for the trip, the other half of the villainous brotherhood being left in the subterranean stronghold of the lawless organization, which had preyed upon the spacecraft that cruised the seas of space between worlds.

Into the pilot's room of the pirate spacecraft, one of the buccaneers came.

"Is everything aboard ready, Delon?" asked Carconte, turning to the man who had just entered. "Are we prepared?"

"The gravitational spikes are in fine working order, our atom guns have been tested, and the atomic energy deflectors have been overhauled," replied the man.

"What of the radio attachments to the deflector," rasped Hulan, "have they been adjusted as I ordered?"

"To the finest point," replied Delon.

"All right," said Carconte. "Go and tell the men we shall overtake the *Limited* within the next three hours, and be ready to receive and carry out my orders."

Delon hurried from the presence of his two superiors, and now Hulan and Carconte bent their heads together over a black square that showed them a view of the sky. Under the control of Hulan, the plate grew misty, and the scintillating stars, which shone from out the square of blackness depicted by the machine, grew dim. Then, under the adjustment of the human robot, the plate grew clear once more to reveal a certain section of the skies through which a spaceship raced, the *Interplanetary Limited* bound for Mars.

The little dot upon the screen grew in proportion as the pirate craft rapidly overtook the *Interplanetary Limited*. His hand at the radio controls, Hulan with a wicked, malicious grin upon his pale countenance, reached across the intervening distance of space to neutralize the *Limited's* propulsion charges of atomic energy, and slow it down. Speedily, they approached close to the great liner of space.

"They have stopped completely now," said Hulan. We shall have to maneuver alongside them."

"Get into communication with the ship," ordered Carconte, "and tell them that if they don't give in at once, we'll fire a hole right through them, and let their air leak out into space; then we shall board them and take what we want."

"Why not do that anyhow?" queried Hulan. "Would it not be the most efficient manner in which to dispose of them, and save time and trouble?"

"No," replied Carconte flatly. "Perhaps we may find additions to our ranks among the crew—who knows—and we can use a few more men. Then, too, you remarked the other day that you were in need of human material for experiment in your laboratory. Here is your chance—and Hulan, you forget that Zind is aboard the *Limited*."

"What you say concerning my experiments is true," replied Hulan, "but in the case of needing more men, I believe we have plenty to keep in hand now. As for Zind, he has a space suit with him in case of just such an emergency."

"Anyhow," stated Carconte, thrusting aside all argument, "we shall take them alive—unless they are too stubborn to surrender voluntarily."

"Put the ray gun across their lower stabilizer fin," ordered the pirate chief. "Let them know we mean business and want to come to terms immediately."

Off the side of the pirate space flyer from the moon, the ray of light shot forth from one of the long, slender cylinders that studded the sides of the craft. A long, ragged rent appeared in the stabilizer fin that kept the space liner on an even keel while flying through the atmosphere of the planets. The ray had penetrated the huge sheet of metal to display its powers to the crew and passengers of the *Interplanetary Limited*. Carconte wished to frighten them into immediate surrender with a demonstration of the ray that Hulan had invented and perfected.

Hulan now spoke to them in his crisp, monotonous voice, which commanded them in imperious tones to stand by without resistance on pain of immediate death to all.

"Passengers and crew of the *Interplanetary Limited*, we are the moon pirates, and we want the treasure you have aboard your ship. One of your passengers also carries valuable bonds that we desire. We are making no terms with you except that if you do not remain passive we shall use the terrible ray gun upon the sides of your ship just as we did upon the stabilizer fin, the results of which you have witnessed. You have a chance for life, if you give in to us quietly, but if we meet with resistance it's certain death to you all! We shall give you ten minutes according to Earth time to come to a decision and await our orders..."

Instantly a pandemonium of chaos reigned within the *Interplanetary Limited,* and everyone attempted to speak at once, offering exciting suggestions.

"Put on all speed, and get out of the reach of their ray!"

"It's death for us all!"

"They'll burn a hole through our ship. Surrender at once!"

"It's worse than death to surrender!"

"Fight them…"

"They want the gold and bonds—give them to the pirates and we shall be saved!"

"I shall not give them these bonds," refused Clarkford.

"Stop this idle bickering!" shouted Jan Trenton, leaping to a table top where he could command the attention of all. "We have only ten minutes to reach a decision before that deadly ray burns a hole through the side of our space flyer! You know what that means—our air will rush out into the vacuum, and we shall suffocate and freeze! We cannot get away from them, for our ship is held within a magnetic grip. We must listen to these robbers of space, who call themselves the moon pirates, and accede to their present demands. Remember, my friends, while there is life there is hope…"

The ringing words of the head pilot of the *Limited* brought a semblance of order to the passengers and crew who were faced with an unprecedented occurrence since the innovation of space flying. The activities of the moon pirates had been so sly and efficient that to date none of the three worlds dreamed that such an organization existed, and the few small space flyers that had come up missing had been laid to meteors or faulty mechanism.

"RADIO Earth for help!" advised Brentley.

"With our equipment all dead from the influence of those devils?" retorted Trenton.

Brentley lapsed into silence.

"It would be best to surrender at once," advised Balfour a bit nervously.

"Doesn't look as if there's anything else to do, as far as I can see," remarked Sorelle. "This is a new one on me—moon pirates!"

"But what will they do with us?" protested Crayton.

"And my daughter?" added Clarkford.

At the business man's words, the face of Jan Trenton paled slightly, while Sorelle clenched his fists and bit his lower lip.

"Four minutes more," announced Brentley.

"They want the gold, platinum and bonds," remarked Balfour. "Probably after we give them those articles we shall be allowed to go upon our way unmolested."

"Ask them if upon receipt of the treasure they will allow us our freedom!" snapped Sorelle.

Jan Trenton did as he was bid, and then turned around to the group once more with the cryptic reply of the moon pirates.

"They say that unless we follow their directions within three minutes, their ray will penetrate our hull..."

"We shall have to depend upon their mercy," stated Sorelle.

"There's evidently no other way out of it," agreed the astronaut.

"What are their instructions?" asked Balfour.

"To allow them to come up alongside of us without attempting to ram or elude them in any manner," replied Jan Trenton. To do so would seal our fate. They expect no treachery."

"Well, tell them—quick, then," quavered the Martian botanist, Professor Crayton, as he consulted the time.

The astronaut communicated the consent of those aboard the *Interplanetary Limited* to comply with the pirates' demands, and they awaited the next maneuvers of the moon-craft, with doubt in their hearts, gambling with the outcome of the affair.

Had they seen the cruel, thin lipped smile of the aluminum-headed Hulan, or the broad wicked grin of Carconte, or heard the triumphant yells from the villainous crew, their hopes would have died within them. Could they have seen beyond the metal skull of Hulan into the active brain of the machine man; who had been brought back to life without a soul, they would have frozen with stark horror, welcoming the merciful oblivion of the yellow ray from the pirate craft.

The *Jolly Roger* swung slowly toward them until with a dull thud and a shiver of the *Limited's* larger proportion's the two space flyers came into close contact.

"Keep away from the point of contact if you value your lives!" came the warning from the moon pirates.

The occupants of the interplanetary ship kept at a discreet distance from the point where the hulls of the two ships had touched. It was well that they did, for a low hum sounded in their ears, a slight vibration manifesting itself throughout the spaceship, tickling the soles of their feet where they rested on the floor. A dull glow spread its weird effulgence upon the side of the huge liner in a rectangle large enough for a person to stand upright against. Gradually the iridescent tints of blue, orange and red predominated over the natural color of the spaceship's interior, and the rectangle of changing colors died away with the cessation of the humming, vibration. There before their astonished eyes, hermetically connected with a square protuberance of the pirate craft, was a rectangular hole in the side of the spaceship. A panel slid aside at the farther end of the protuberance, and two men walked through the connecting corridor into the *Interplanetary Limited.*

ONE of the men caused the passengers and crew of the spaceship to gasp in sudden awe and astonishment at his weird, unearthly appearance. A shining aluminum cranium, beginning just above the eyes and covering the upper part of his head to a position just below his metal ears surmounted a pale countenance marked with a cruel smile of intellectual superiority. It was a smile of contempt, amusement and satisfaction. His mechanical limbs and steel fingers completed the amazing details of his body. The other man was a bald, short, thick ruffian whose wicked eyes gleamed as they rapidly took in the group before him. Behind the two there pushed a motley horde of ill assorted, villainous looking, unkempt ruffians who brandished atom-pistols and other weapons, forcing their way along behind the two foremost men.

"Nez Hulan!" ejaculated Professor Crayton at sight of the human robot who had lain dead in space for three long years.

"My Professor Crayton," rasped the unpleasant voice of the mechanical limbed man with a sneering smirk of recognition. "This is indeed a pleasure which I would not have foregone for anything."

"Zind! Come here, you precious rascal, and tell me which of these men carries the bonds!" remarked the verbose Carconte.

The assembled group of passengers and crew gasped in surprise as the dark-faced Balfour stepped forward from their ranks and stood beside the pirate chieftain.

"That man," he said, pointing to Clarkford. "But the twenty million in bonds with their added encumbrance of cashing them before trouble starts is but a drop in the bucket to the wealth this ship carries! It's beyond your wildest dream, Carconte. Imagine it if you can…five-hundred-million dollars worth of gold, platinum and precious stones!"

The eyes of Carconte nearly popped from his head at the announcement of Zind, previously known to the passengers of the *Interplanetary Limited* as Mr. Balfour, traveling to Mars as a scientific representative of a Venerian concern. A wild yell of approval broke forth from the uncouth ranks of the pirates who had poured into the craft behind their leaders. Even the self-confident, sedate expression of Hulan was upset by the startling news that a half billion lay within their reach.

"We are the sons of fortune!" shouted Carconte with vehemence.

"And what of these?" asked Hulan pointing a steel finger towards the group of crew and passengers with supercilious attitude. "Before we remove the treasure to our own ship, we must dispose of the passengers."

"RUN them into our ship and lock them up," ordered Carconte. "We'll deal with them later, after the treasure is safely within the *Jolly Roger* and this interplanetary spacecraft is put where it won't be found. Come, you laggards, put these people where they belong, and slit their throats if they give you any trouble!"

Carconte motioned the men forward, and the pirates of the moon seized upon the luckless passengers none too gently and escorted them along the passage into the *Jolly Roger*, prodding them with atom guns or whatever object they carried. As Suzette Clarkford walked past the pirate leader, Carconte reached forward and grasped the girl by the shoulder. She faced him, her startled eyes looking straight into those of the brigand who avidly drank in the beauty of her face.

"I'll take care of you later, my pretty one," he promised. "Never fear—you shall not meet the same fate as the others."

The girl shuddered. Hulan frowned. Clarkford twisted about in the grasp of two burly ruffians in a vain effort to come back to the side of his daughter. Jan Trenton, who was following the girl through the opening in the spaceship halted momentarily, and the two pirates who were escorting him, being amused by the actions of their leader, did not urge his lagging footsteps until the girl had passed into the corridor. Upon Carconte's villainous face there set an expression of anticipation, not born of the greed for gold.

Clarkford, his daughter, Professor Crayton, Bret Sorelle and the crew of the ill-fated spaceship were herded into a compartment of the raiding spacecraft. Here, they could look from a series of narrow windows at the *Interplanetary Limited* from which the pirates were removing the treasure and such other articles as caught their fancy.

Suzette Clarkford was a brave young lady; but being a woman, and in the face of such hopeless, distressing circumstances, she broke down and cried in the protective hollow of her father's arms.

"Don't anyone try to pass this doorway," advised one of the pirates. "There's no lock or door to keep you in, but whoever wishes to pass through this blue light is welcome to do so."

The man pressed a button across the corridor from the room in which the captives were gathered, and there sprang into sight another product of the scientific genius of Nez Hulan, a close set arrangement of violet shafts of light spread across the doorway. One of the crew of the *Interplanetary Limited* thrust a hand curiously towards the violet light before Jan Trenton could jerk him away from, the doorway, but not before the tips of two of the man's fingers had been thrust into the rays of deep violet hue.

"Keep away from that, if you value your life!" exclaimed the astronaut. "It's more effective in keeping us imprisoned here than a locked door!"

The man now stared aghast at the tips of his two fingers which had turned black under the exposure to the violet shafts of light. He complained of no pain, but as he took the injured members between the fingers of his other hand, the black tips fell away to the floor like charred wood.

"What if you had stuck your head through instead of your fingers?" remarked Sorelle.

From then on, every one of the captives kept at a respectful distance from the doorway of their cell.

The pirates were engaged in removing the shipment of gold, platinum and precious stones from the *Interplanetary Limited*. During the transfer of the vast riches, their prisoners within the pirate craft saw none of their captors.

Suddenly a cry from one of the crew of the interplanetary spaceship drew their attention to the windows of their cell where a view could be had of the spaceship.

"We're doomed!" exclaimed the man. "We shall never escape them. Look at that!"

Everyone looked—and what they saw chilled them with the horror of the situation. The yellow ray from the *Jolly Roger* played over the side of the ill-fated space liner, tearing great gaping holes in the side of the ship, which now had been thoroughly looted by the moon pirates."

"THEY'RE destroying the *Limited!*" swore Sorelle. "The dirty dogs!"

"We'll be taken prisoners, that's sure," said Trenton.

"To the moon…" ejaculated Professor Crayton dismally.

"Isn't there some way we can buy them off—or do something to make them let us go?" pleaded Brentley, terror stricken.

"What would we do, now that our ship's destroyed?" asked one of the crew.

"But—but—they're apt to kill us all!" replied the shaking voice of the frightened co-pilot.

"You mean that seeing they have the treasure they will cover up their foul deed by—"

A terrific explosion cut short the words of Clarkford, and those within the pirate spaceship felt a quiver run through the entire craft. The eyes of the group gazed in astonishment at the spot where the *Interplanetary Limited* had been; it was gone!

"What—what happened?" questioned Professor Crayton. "It all occurred so quickly that I didn't see it..."

"They have sent the *Interplanetary Limited*, or what was left of it, speeding off into space out of the solar system so that their black deed will remain a mystery, and minimize the chances of being found out," announced Jan Trenton. "The question now concerns what they will do with us."

"It's a cinch they're not going to let any of us return to the three worlds—not after this," stated Sorelle.

"But what will they do to us?" asked Professor Crayton, his voice truly shaken.

"That you will soon find out, my Professor," rasped an unpleasant voice from the corridor.

The four passengers and the crew of the *Interplanetary Limited,* the latter numbering eight inclusive of the two pilots, Trenton and Brentley, turned quickly away from their places at the window from which they had been looking out into space.

The violet shafts of light within the doorway had disappeared and in their place stood the human-mechanical demon, Nez Hulan, while behind him the leering countenance of Carconte peered over his shoulder. A huge scar-faced brute of a man accompanied them, and aside from the three there were no others in sight. The voice of Hulan continued.

"Yes, Professor Crayton, you will soon find out what's to become of you. You are to serve an illustrious purpose in the interests of science, and together, you and I, we shall work out an interesting experiment I have had in mind for some time. Do you remember Professor Climm at Fomar?"

"Why, yes," replied Professor Crayton reminiscently. "He was the man with whose murder you were charged—that is, one of the *men*."

"No—no, my dear Crayton," protested Hulan, his eyes gleaming in amusement. "The unfortunate case of Climm was merely the result of one of my experiments. If you remember, Climm occupied the room across from mine, and one morning he was found lying dead upon the floor of his chamber, the bones of his body being entirely decomposed."

"From that infernal machine in your room," accused Professor Crayton who had for the moment forgotten his situation, and whose voice arose in righteous wrath.

"But anyway," continued the human robot, waving aside the accusation with an impatient gesture of his steel arm, "that is all immaterial to the subject I have in mind. Do you remember his successful experiment with the dog, in which he decapitated the animal and kept it alive for an indefinite period of time, the head in one section of the laboratory and the body in another?"

"Yes—I saw the animal," replied Crayton. "It seems that by an elaborate system of wiring and tubes connecting the two widely separated sections of the creature's anatomy he kept the dog alive for some time—until tiring of the experiment he killed the animal."

"I know," said Hulan. "I worked with him upon the experiment, and aided him in the perfection of several principles regarding it."

"Yes," followed Crayton.

"You and I are going to conduct that very same experiment just as soon as we get back to the moon," announced Hulan, cryptically.

"WE are?" said the perplexed professor.

"Yes!" clicked the mechanical-limbed man.

"With a dog?" asked the professor curiously.

"No...a man!" was the ominous retort.

"But, that's murder!" cried Crayton in alarm.

"Not from a scientific point of view, my professor," answered the mastermind of the moon pirates.

"But who will submit to such an experiment?" queried the professor weakly, plainly aghast at the man's inhuman attitude, with its cruel disregard for human life and suffering.

"You will!" snapped the human-robot with terrible finality in his tone, and a merciless sneer of contempt upon his pale features.

"No-no-no, not that!" pleaded Crayton, shivering so dreadfully that he tottered weakly to his knees and sought support by grasping a nearby table. "I'll do—anything but that!"

The man continued to babble incoherently for his life, while Nez Hulan stood before him with a cruel, malicious smile upon his face. Hulan never laughed, and had he done so it is probable that his laughter would have been more chilling than his smile.

"Enough of this useless talk!" roared Carconte who had tired of the sport of terrorizing his victims. "I want those bonds. Give them to me..."

In view of the fact that resistance was utterly useless and foolhardy, Clarkford immediately handed over the flat bundle of papers he had kept within an inner pocket. Eagerly, the pirate seized them, and gave the bonds a cursory glance, shoving them inside his loose-fitting blouse.

"And now as for the rest of you," continued Carconte, "you have a choice of joining up with us in the brotherhood of our ranks, or else it is death—perhaps worse, if Hulan takes a notion to carve you up!"

"I'll join—I'll join!" shouted Crayton feverishly.

"You'll do nothing!" retorted Carconte. "Your mangy, old carcass wouldn't be worth the room it takes up. Hulan can have you if he wishes!

"Now then, who else will volunteer to join us?"

Hesitatingly, as if a bit uncertain, Brentley and two of the crew stepped forward.

"So…" laughed Carconte. "We have three likely looking chaps who would honor our band with their membership?"

With swift, calculating eyes, the leader of the moon pirates appraised them.

"Very good—all fine material," he said. "Stand aside from the rest."

"What of you?" he asked Sorelle.

"I'll see you in hell first," replied the adventurer, his eyes snapping.

Instead of being angered by the affront, the pirate was amused.

"Here is a man worthy of our mettle. Too bad such a man must die, eh, Hulan?" observed Carconte.

"Leave him to me," retorted the aluminum-headed man. "A slight operation of the brain will cure him—and if you desire him, why he shall become one of us, and a fine pirate he should make."

AND so Sorelle, with Jan Trenton and another reluctant member of the crew, were ranged alongside of Brentley and the two who had volunteered with the co-pilot.

"The rest of you die!" said Carconte. "Except the lady. I shall attend to her as soon as we reach the moon."

"Save that man," said Hulan pointing a steel finger at Clarkford. "I wish to experiment upon him also."

Suzette Clarkford gave out a shriek and fainted into the arms of Jan Trenton, who leaped forward and caught her as she fell.

"That leaves two of you for the tube," said Carconte, and then he turned to the scar-faced villain who stood silently eyeing the group of prisoners. "Have the ship stopped at once, and the gun prepared; we have two reluctant passengers who wish to leave."

CHAPTER FIVE
The Emblem of Death

THE man hurried away. The two remaining members of the crew who had been left, following the selection for the experiments of Hulan and the additions to the ranks of the moon pirates, stood bravely with set, white faces. They were fully prepared for whatever terrible end the pirate leader had in store for them. He had mentioned a gun. Were they to be shot to infinitesimal fragments from the mouth of a cannon? It was not long before they found out.

"Come along," ordered Carconte." All of you..."

The pirate chief started through the doorway, and the iron arm of Hulan silently beckoned for the rest to follow. The dozen prisoners from the *Interplanetary Limited* filed from the room out into the corridor, down which they walked for a short distance, until Carconte led the way into another chamber of the spacecraft. Before them lay a mass of machinery and equipment.

"Seven hundred years ago," said Carconte, "the pirates disposed of all those for whom they had no use by making them walk the plank into the ocean. Sometimes they tied them to the mast and blew up the ship—that, too, was a good way, but here in space we are under different conditions in a far advanced age of progress. Planks and watery depths are not associated with space flyers. Instead of the plank we have this."

Carconte pointed to a long cylinder that projected through the side of the spaceship.

"Attend the gun, Terseg!" ordered Carconte to a man with squint eyes and a long peaked nose.

The pirate sprang forward and twisted several levers at the base of the cylinder. The top opened to reveal a compartment seven feet long and three feet wide within the interior of the cylinder.

"This is the gun," said Carconte. "You all know the destructiveness of the atom's explosions within a confined space. An object placed within this cylinder is disintegrated within the short space of a few minutes by atomic combustion and radioactivity, being reduced to its component elements, which are then ejected into space. Which of you two men wish to be the first?"

The pirate chief grinned evilly, while Hulan's face wore its usual sardonic smile, possibly seasoned at this moment with an expression of anticipation, for his usual impassive face wore very few varieties of expressions at any time. The six or seven pirates within the room wore broad grins as if the disintegration of two of their fellow men was a huge joke.

One of the men stepped forward.

"Get in!" said Terseg, pointing to the cylinder's compartment.

The man lay face upward at full length within the cylinder's interior, his white, ashen countenance portraying his fatalistic resignation to the unavoidable hopelessness of the situation. With the jerk of a lever. Terseg closed the upper half of the hollow cylinder down over the recumbent man and humanity had its last view of a brave engineer of an interplanetary flyer. Turning a wheel upon the base of the cylinder, Terseg consulted a dial upon the wall to one side of the gun.

"WHEN the needle of that dial goes all the way around once, it will signify that the man is no more, and that the gun is loaded for its shot into space," elucidated Carconte for the benefit of the horrified group of prisoners.

Slowly the needle crept around the dial, finally, though it seemed ages for those who were looking upon it for the first time, the needle completed the circuit of the dial.

"Watch the muzzle of the gun," directed Carconte, waving a hand towards the window of the craft through which the extremity of the cylinder could be seen.

Like an irresistible magnet the muzzle of the disintegrator gun drew the attention of all as they stared in horrid fascination at the anticipated spectacle.

"Get ready, Terseg," ordered Carconte.

The Terseg placed a hand upon the knob that studded the wall alongside of the dial.

"Fire!"

From the mouth of the gun there burst a streak of iridescent flame, and the occupants of the pirate craft were conscious of a slight concussion, which shook the space flyer with a vague, perceptible tremor. A silent tribute enfolded the captives. A wicked laugh from Carconte shattered the silence.

"You're next!" he motioned to the remaining victim. "Get in there and see if you can make a prettier flash of fire!"

Again his iniquitous laugh sounded throughout the chamber, and was joined by the laughter and chuckles of his men. The second man stepped forward, took a farewell look out of the window of the flyer at a little red planet whose dull eye shone steadily from out of the infinitude of space, and then prepared for his dissolution and projection into eternity. Again Terseg closed the cylinder upon the victim of the moon pirates, and again there followed the long, drawn out pause of a few minutes while the needle crawled around the dial. Then came the iridescent streak of light sending the atomic remains of the second man off into the stellar void between worlds to join those of the first.

"And what have we left?" asked Carconte more to himself than to anyone else. "You want these two for experiments, do you not?"

The pirate chief pointed to Clarkford and Crayton, turning to Hulan for confirmation of the latter's intentions.

"Yes," replied Hulan.

"And these," said Carconte, pointing to Brentley and two of the crew, "are the volunteers."

"Those other three must be operated upon to remove the unwillingness from their brains before they will make good pirates," said Hulan, pointing to Sorelle, Trenton, and the remaining member of the crew who had all preferred death to joining the outlawed ranks of the moon pirates. Because of physical capability, they were desired by Carconte and his mechanical limbed confederate.

"And the woman," said Hulan, the cruel lines of his mouth twisting downward. "The atom gun is ready for her."

"No," said the scar-faced brute who had listened to the words of Carconte and Hulan, "I'll give half my gold to the general fund if she may be spared to me!"

His evil face with the long red furrow plainly writ across his grizzled visage beneath the stubble of unkempt beard, peered up at the pirate chieftain, while his fingers twitched nervously as he stole covetous glances at Suzette Clarkford who had now emerged from her faint.

"You will, will you?" roared the enraged Carconte. "So—you would aspire to own the woman, would you—and give half of your gold for her? What makes you think you are going to get any of the gold? After looking at you, I believe the lady would much prefer the disintegrator gun."

Scar-face wilted beneath the torrent of abuse that his superior had heaped upon him, as well as from the yells of derision and laughter from the other pirates.

"I HAVE her fate all settled, and it will be a far better one than our considerate Scar-face offers. She shall not be sacrificed to the gun; she will be reserved to serve a more noble purpose." This last sentence the boastful pirate leader directed at Hulan.

Suzette Clarkford shuddered at the three plans that had been outlined for her by the pirates, and now the disintegrator gun appeared to her not as a terrible weapon to be classified with the iron maiden and such other damnable creations of antiquity, but as a machine of merciful deliverance. She envied the two who had previously been shot into oblivion by the disintegrator gun, and could realize that theirs had been the most compassionate fate to be meted out at the hands of the moon pirates.

"And now, you three volunteers," said Carconte, pointing to Brentley and his two associates, "before you take the oath of the brotherhood, and become moon pirates, you must receive our insignia. When we reach the rendezvous upon the moon, you will have the oath administered to you. Hulan, you and Luddock brand these three men with the insignia. The unwilling cannot receive it until their brains have been slightly altered under the capable hands of Hulan."

A tall, lanky pirate, evidently Luddock, beckoned to the three men who, actuated by cowardice and disloyalty, had agreed to evade any severe consequences to themselves by voluntarily becoming buccaneers of space. Luddock led them to a complicated piece of apparatus, which arose shoulder high from the floor. Hulan took a position behind it where he tinkered a moment. A strange light enveloped the machine and then Luddock spoke to Brentley.

"Shove that sleeve of your right arm back, and put your arm through that hole."

The pirate pointed to a circular, padded hole in the machine. Brentley did as he was directed, though a bit hesitant as if he feared something. Shaking, and slowly, he inserted his arm into the machine.

"To the full length!" commanded Carconte, looking on.

The awed co-pilot of the *Interplanetary Limited* did as he was instructed. Upon the other side of the machine Hulan pressed a few buttons and levers, the light, of an unnamable tint, gaining intensity. The face of Brentley underwent no sudden change. Only a look of stupid surprise slowly mantled his countenance, replacing the look of fear and dread as if something he had expected to occur had not happened.

"Remove your arm," said Hulan after a moment or so.

Brentley did so, looking hastily at it as he withdrew the arm. From between the wrist and forearm there glared at him the black silhouette of a skull and cross bones, the emblem of piracy and death! Beneath this were the outlines of a crescent moon.

"A GOOD impression," remarked Luddock. "Let's see how the other side came out."

Taking Brentley's arm, the pirate turned it around and there to Brentley's surprise was another skull and cross bones with the accompanying moon's crescent.

"Two of them!" cried Brentley.

"No, one of them," corrected Luddock. "It goes all of the way through your arm—even through the bone."

"You are all finished for the time being," said Carconte to Brentley. "Hurry up, you two; finish off those others, and we'll get back to the moon."

It took but a short time to place the insignia of the moon pirates upon the other two and the pirates all rolled back their right arm sleeves to display the devilish emblems that adorned their forearms. Below the skull and cross bones of some of the pirates, there was outlined a quarter moon while a few bore full moons.

"Those quarter moons and full moons are overprinted upon the crescents following some special mark of service or bravery," explained Carconte. "They are not conferred aboard ship, but only in the recesses of our caverns, which you will shortly see. Zind is to have his crescent replaced by a quarter moon just as soon as our ship reaches home."

"Let us get under way," suggested Hulan. "This is a bad place in which to be caught."

"Any place is bad enough," said Carconte. The sooner we get back, the less chances we have of being seen by the telescopes of the three worlds."

The moon pirates headed for the Earth's satellite.

Their hideout, discreetly located upon the side of the moon that never faces Earth, was out of sight of all prying telescopes. The prisoners, with the exceptions of Brentley, and the two members of the crew who had joined the ranks of the moon pirates, were returned once more to their original cell, from where they watched the descent to the moon. They were all in rather gloomy spirits, especially Professor Crayton who raved and babbled incoherently.

"Don't give up hope," reassured Trenton to the girl who was sobbing gently. "Those moon pirates went a step too far when they picked on the *Limited* to rob and capture its passengers. It's less than fifteen minutes ride from the Earth to the moon, and just as soon as it's found that the

Interplanetary Limited has mysteriously disappeared without a radio communication of any kind, there will be a space-wide search to the boundaries of the solar system with powerful telescopes, and when they do not pick out our craft, or do not hear from it, the matter will be thoroughly investigated."

"By that time it will be too late," said Clarkford. "They will have no more idea of where to look for us, or realize that we are so close to the Earth, than we knew beforehand that there was such a lawless band as the moon pirates."

THE logic of Clarkford's reasoning silenced the young astronaut for a moment and then he spoke.

"Don't be so pessimistic. I have been in tighter jams than this before—and I'm still here," he reminded them.

"I believe in your philosophy Trenton!" said Sorelle. "What we must do is not abandon hope, but watch for an opportunity and hope for the best."

"They can't have my head—I won't let them!" raved Crayton from a stool where he sat with his head in his hands, staring wild-eyed at the ceiling. "I'm not going to a living death—Climm was right, that's what it was, and he put the dog out of its misery!"

"Poor man," said the girl, "he has gone demented since talking with that terrible machine man!"

"And I little blame him," observed Sorelle, gazing in pity at the botanist whose mental faculties had been reduced to a wreck through the abject terror inspired in him by the human robot. "That man would give almost anyone the creeps."

"I wonder which of those craters is our destination," observed Quenden, the remaining member of the crew who had not voluntarily joined the ranks of the pirates, and who had escaped the disintegrator gun through a desirability on the part of the moon pirates to alter his intentions by a slight brain operation.

"I, too, wonder," mused Sorelle as the two gazed down upon the pockmarked surface of the great, airless globe.

"We are descending rather rapidly," said Trenton. "See how fast the moon is growing in proportion. Such a speed would be impossible if the moon possessed an atmosphere. It's rushing right up at us!"

"Have you ever been upon the moon before?" queried Sorelle.

"Yes—many times," replied Trenton.

"Do you think they will put us under the knife as soon as we get there?" remarked Quenden. "I have no desire for them to work on my brain."

"I can't say," said Trenton. "I imagine they will give us a few days in which to change our minds and become moon pirates without the necessity of a surgical operation."

"Can they accomplish it?" asked Clarkford.

"I believe that Hulan can accomplish almost anything that's devilish," replied Jan Trenton. "He has the mind of a fiend…"

"That comes of bringing the dead back to life," said Quenden cryptically. "It was too bad that the meteor didn't destroy his head entirely, instead of only fracturing his skull that time."

THE girl screamed suddenly, electrifying the group of men into action.

"Save him—somebody! Save him quick!"

There before their eyes across the room stood the Martian botanist, muttering to himself, and advancing to the doorway across which the deadly shafts of violet light played constantly. His mutterings rose to a yell, and his eyes blazed with a strange light as he ran for the doorway.

"Nez Hulan shall not have me!" Crayton screamed in a shrill voice. "I'll escape him!"

Jan Trent and Bret Sorelle leaped forward simultaneously to drag back the crazed professor from the doom of the deep violet rays of destroying intensity. Both were too late; for with a final, despairing wail, the Martian professor plunged headlong through the shafts of light to the floor of the corridor beyond the doorway.

A number of the pirates, hearing the commotion, came running down the passage. Hulan and Carconte soon appeared.

"There goes one of your experiments," said Carconte, pointing to the slumped form of Professor Crayton whose face had turned black.

Hulan gave the corpse a sharp, disgusted kick with his foot. The body crumpled up into a mound of black dust and charred clothing.

"I can use another of them," he frowned. "Clean up this mess!"

Some of the pirates immediately obeyed the order of the aluminum-skulled man who was the next in command under Carconte.

"Turn off those rays in the doorway, too," said Carconte, "before more of them cheat us of their lives. I'll place a guard over them until we leave the ship, which won't be long. We are coming down now."

"We haven't searched them for weapons yet," observed one of the pirates.

"True," remarked Carconte as if the idea had not occurred to him before. "Search them, though I believe they carry no weapons, for space liner passengers rarely carry them. Be sure to search that astronaut, though, he might have a gun on him if any of them have."

A pirate felt carefully about the clothes of each of the captives. One dark-skinned, villainous looking fellow approached the girl, who shrank from him.

"I have no weapons!" she said in alarm.

Still the man came forward to where she had backed up against the wall. Swiftly he ran his hands over the pockets of her outer garments in search of weapons, and when he had satisfied himself that she carried none, he drew her toward him, his eyes inflamed with reckless passion.

JAN TRENTON was nearest the girl, and the first thing the pirate knew, the fist of the young astronaut had crashed into his face, and he was sitting upon the floor. With murder in his heart, the man jerked a ray gun from his pocket and prepared to burn a hole through the vitals of the astronaut.

As the enraged pirate sprang forward to consummate the dastardly act, a set of steel fingers closed upon his windpipe and a cold voice hissed in his ear:

"Drop that gun!"

The tightening fingers threatened to snap the neck of the pirate, and the man, gasping for breath and with fear and surprise in his heart, dropped the pistol. Hulan had saved the life of Jan Trenton not for any humane reason, but for the benefit of the moon pirates, or perhaps to meet a more terrible end at the hands of the machine man himself. The face of the pirate wilted with fear, and his countenance grew livid as he looked into the eyes of Hulan—the very eyes of death itself!

"You fool!" his metallic voice clicked as he cast the terror-stricken pirate from him. "Do you want to kill another, after we have already lost one?"

The man with the aluminum braincase and the rubber heart now turned to his pirate chief.

"You see, Carconte, what I told you about the woman is true. Already she's bringing us trouble. It would have been far better to have consigned her to the gun!"

"She'll bring no trouble when we reach the moon," grinned Carconte. "I have a special place for her within my private quarters, where she shall not be bothered by the men. There will be no more trouble."

Hulan, however, shook his metal capped head in a dismal gesture of hopeless resignation, which portended grim forebodings of the evil that would come to them. Women, he had always maintained, brought only misfortune and disaster to such as the moon pirates.

CHAPTER SIX
Imprisoned in the Moon

THE two pirate leaders left the presence of their captives to superintend the descent of the *Jolly Roger* into the moon crater, leaving a guard of several of the lunar buccaneers by the doorway of the chamber leading into the long corridor of the spaceship.

Now that they were alone once more, Suzette approached the young astronaut who had so nobly defended her at the risk of sudden death to himself. Placing her hand in his, the girl turned her sweet face up to him, and her pretty blue eyes gazed into those of Jan Trenton.

"How can I ever thank you?"

"I couldn't stand by and see those brutes maltreat you," he said, placing a hand softly upon her wavy brown hair. "None of us would let them do that, and at the time the responsibility fell to me in view of the fact that I was closest to you."

"Stay close to me," she whispered, as she shuddered in recollection of the attempt upon the part of the uncouth, villainous pirate to seize her.

"I shall," he replied. "Don't give up hope until the last moment; then if it is necessary, swallow this."

He held a small capsule out to the girl.

"What is it?" she asked.

"Radium," he said. "When the container is dissolved, loosing the destroying element within, death is nearly instantaneous. Take it; it's the last one I have."

"But you?" she asked.

"There are other ways for us men to die. Being a woman and under such circumstances, you have no other choice."

She smiled wanly.

"But wait until the final moment," he added, "until the last vestige of hope is gone before giving yourself over to death."

"Thank you so much," she replied. "I feel a great deal better now."

"We're descending the crater!" exclaimed Sorelle from the window where he, Trenton, Clarkford, and Quenden were watching the maneuvers of the spaceship in its approach to the moon's pitted surface.

Jan Trenton and Suzette Clarkford now turned their attention to the interior of the crater into which they were gradually sinking. The rugged walls of the depression cleft here and there with gaunt, black shadows, swung slowly past the windows of the spacecraft, as it sank deeper and deeper into the moon pit. The sunshine threw its dazzling glow upon the side of the moon crater at which they were looking; the shadows stamped in sharp relief through the lack of an existent atmosphere to diffuse and spread the light.

"How weird and solemn it all is," said the girl. "I have never been to the moon before..."

"The moon does have rather a strange, depressing effect upon one," said Sorelle.

"And especially so under the present circumstances," observed Clarkford gloomily.

With a sudden cessation that was startling, the glow of sunlight disappeared, leaving the captives to stare abstractedly into the Stygian gloom of the lower depths of the crater. Complete blackness surrounded them; they had passed below the level that marked the extremity of the sun's rays within the deep confines of the pit. Then there was a sudden illumination that dispelled the darkness as the lights of the *Jolly Roger* played about upon the rough walls of the pit, guiding the pirate craft to its destination upon the floor of the crater far below.

Presently they came to rest, presumably upon the bottom of the pit, several miles below the moon's surface.

"Have we arrived?" queried the girl.

"I don't know," replied the young astronaut. "We've stopped moving."

"Look!" exclaimed Quenden, pointing to a huge, round cave's mouth that lay before them at the extremity of the crater's interior. "I wonder where that goes?"

"We shall soon find out," said Sorelle, as with a slight jerk the spacecraft moved slowly toward the dark opening that, as they approached it, yawned larger and larger like the cavernous mouth of an abysmal creature born of a fantastic dream.

The opening loomed larger, received them, and then they were engulfed within its interior, which led downwards on a gradual incline. The tunnel extended for nearly a half mile, the slant of the great underground shaft bearing the craft of the moon pirates deeper into the bowels of the lunar satellite. Eventually, they halted before a smooth wall of rock, its polished surface contrasting strangely beside the rough, jagged interior of the tunnel. To the surprised eyes of the prisoners aboard the *Jolly Roger,* this rose slowly upward, revealing the confines of a cavern beyond. Into this, the spacecraft once more proceeded upon its way. Behind it, the great wall of rock closed gently, hermetically sealing the rocky chamber of the air-lock cavern of the moon pirates.

A pause of a few minutes was necessary for the vacuum of the air lock to be filled with atmosphere that was manufactured by the moon pirates, and then farther on, another wall of rock arose to allow them further entrance. They continued their progress, the walls of the air lock closing behind them. From here on, the tunnel was brightly illuminated, and finally terminated in a subterranean hangar for a number of ships of various nondescript types, which had been captured by the moon pirates and brought to this secret recluse of the lawless buccaneers of space.

Foremost in the minds of the captives from the *Interplanetary Limited* was the conjecture concerning what had become of the crews and passengers of these space flyers, which suggested tragic encounters with the moon pirates in the seas of space between the orbits of Mars and Venus. What a story they could relate if they were only gifted with speech. It would be a tale of horror and bloodshed, of pillage and murder, of incarceration and torture, of terrible deeds and fates meted out to helpless captives by the poisoned intellect of Hulan's perverted genius!

"Why didn't they take our ship and bring it here too?" queried Clarkford.

"The tunnel isn't large enough for it to enter," replied Quenden. "This ship just about fits the tunnel nicely, and if you remember, the *Interplanetary Limited* was about twice as large as this pirate craft."

"Look!" exclaimed Jan Trenton pointing excitedly at one of the assembled spaceships that were scattered about the broad cavern. "There's the *Antarian,* the small spacecraft that disappeared over a year ago, and trace of which could never be found. The disappearance aroused the wonder and curiosity of three worlds, and to this day it has remained unsolved. These devils were responsible for that too!"

"Were there people aboard?" asked Suzette Clarkford.

"Yes," answered the astronaut, "and that's why it aroused such a furor for a short time. An important government official of the Martian city of Heddux was aboard, and quite an extensive search was made, but no trace of the ship could be found."

"Which goes to show just how much chance we have of being rescued," observed Clarkford dejectedly.

"I remember about the unexplained mystery of the space flyer, the *Antarian,*" said Bret Sorelle, reminiscently. "It seems that this Garn Deblette, with two companions, boarded his space flyer for a weekend cruise to Venus, which would include a circumnavigation of the planet. The only solution of the sudden disappearance of the *Antarian* that could have been plausible, and sounded so, was to the effect that Deblette, in his circumnavigation of Venus, had lost control of his ship, and with a dead broadcaster, with which it had been impossible to summon help, had been drawn into the sun."

"He never even reached Venus," said Quenden, nodding his head towards the *Antarian,* which silently attested to the manner of Deblette's fate along with his two companions. "When his space flyer passed the vicinity of Earth's orbit, he was captured by the moon pirates just as we were."

"A most excellent surmise!" came the startling affirmation from behind the group of captives who were intent upon the bevy of looted spaceships that had fallen prey to the buccaneers of space.

The faces of all turned quickly at the sound of the voice to find Carconte regarding them with amusement.

"And now my guests," he mimicked, "the voyage is ended, and I beg of you to enter my humble domicile."

A guffaw of coarse laughter greeted this buffoonery of the pirate leader as the rows of villainous faces, which peered in at the corridor entrance, received this sally of their chieftain.

"Jezzan, you and Bender act as a guard of honor for these, our guests," indicated Carconte to a pair of trusty villains who were nearest him; the pirate continued the exaggerated politeness that had so amused his cohorts.

The two pirates designated by Carconte led the melancholy group of prisoners from the spaceship out into the cavern of the subterranean moon chambers, and following, came the rest of the motley crew of space brigands led by Carconte. Hulan was not in evidence, having remained within the spaceship on some reason or other.

From the underground hangar of the moon buccaneers, the captives were led into the rendezvous of the pirates to the grand central room. When they had all entered, Carconte addressed the ill-fortuned group of five.

"You are going to be kept together in a cell until tonight, according to Earth time of the western hemisphere, when you shall be judged, and your various fates determined. At our meeting, we shall decide what shall be done with each of you…"

The pirate chief allowed his eyes to rest hungrily upon the shapely form of Suzette Clarkford who instinctively shrank back into the protecting arms of her father. Jan Trenton stepped before the girl, shutting her loveliness from the pirate chief. The young astronaut's eyes bored back into those of the evil, bald headed Carconte. The pirate leader scowled menacingly at this display of valorous defiance on the part of these helpless playthings of fate, whose several destinies had converged to bring them here together within the merciless clutches of these twenty-sixth century pirates. The scowl upon Carconte's unlovely visage turned to one of contemptuous amusement, as the humor of the situation struck him.

"Until tonight, then," said Carconte, as he motioned for the pirates to take the five captives to their temporary confinement.

The two pirates, Bender and Jezzan, led the way. Three more of the space buccaneers followed them. Through a long, winding corridor they were led, and then they entered upon a square room with gray, gloomy walls, which were illuminated by means of a preparation that had been applied to the surface. It was a dim, somber light, which spread its gray, melancholy glow upon the cold walls of the chamber in the moon's interior. Bringing them here, the pirates left them to the silence of the place whose sepulchral drabness lent it an air of oppressiveness, reminding one of the tomb.

"What a terrible room!" shuddered the girl.

"It isn't very cheerful," agreed Sorelle, glancing around at the bare walls of the dimly lit moon chamber.

"Are they going to leave us unguarded?" queried Clarkford, motioning to the open doorway through which the moon pirates had vanished.

"Probably they know we can't get out, or they would have posted a man nearby," observed Quenden.

"Perhaps we are watched by television," suggested Trenton. "I have an uncanny, restless feeling that there are unseen eyes looking at us."

"What was that noise?" whispered Clarkford, the room echoing to his sibilant intonations.

"The floor's shaking!" announced Quenden.

"It's sinking!" shouted Sorelle in alarm.

As the five gazed around in surprise and bewilderment at the walls and doorway that were gradually sliding upward out of sight, they saw that Sorelle was indeed correct in his assertions that the floor was sinking. About forty feet below its original level the floor of the rocky chamber halted its descent and came to rest.

"What was that for, I wonder?" asked Sorelle.

"It makes an ideal prison," observed Jan Trenton, pointing to the doorway far above their heads. "That's the reason why they omitted the details of leaving a guard for us; it wasn't necessary."

"And when they want us again," offered Quenden, "all they will have to do is to elevate the floor of this chamber once more."

"Exactly," agreed Sorelle.

*　　*　　*

A group of men sat in excited conference in an office of a towering, twenty sixth century skyscraper of New York City. From out of the windows of this office, which was located some hundred and twenty stories above the street, could be seen the thriving heart of the great metropolitan city.

Down in the far off street below, one could perceive the tiny dots, pedestrians, going about their business. No surface vehicles were in evidence, being confined to the subway levels. The air, however, was full of planes, airships and interplanetary flyers that plied at various altitudes, according to their types and business. Numerous landing stages were in evidence in supplement to the five upper levels of all the buildings, which were reserved for both air craft and space flyers, the various types being segregated to certain levels. Along near the fifty story level of the skyscrapers, where the lowest landing stages were located, a network of narrow bridges, which supported municipal radium cars, the public conveyances for the twenty-sixth century New York population, connected the skyscrapers;

Within the office, completely oblivious to the throb of life outside, four men sat in conference, stern faces obsessed with the problem at hand.

The report from Mars brings the information that the *Interplanetary Limited* is overdue, and has not been heard from, and that nowhere can it be seen in space, its entire route having been examined by the telescopes."

"What do the Venerians say?" queried another.

"That the spaceship left Venus at the regular time, bound for Mars with a half billion in gold, platinum and diamonds, and carried a passenger list of five, beside the usual crew of eight."

"It was an express, was it not?"

"It was."

"Then what business had the passengers upon it?"

"There were five people, four men and a girl, who were all vouched for by the Venerian authorities at Deliphon. Had they not taken this express, they would have found it necessary to have waited two days for the next 'passenger' limited to Mars, and none of the five cared to wait that long. There were others who wished to take the express but were denied passage, due to the fact that they had no one to vouch for them."

"And what are we to do?"

"What do you suppose we are to do? We must begin a thorough search at once."

"In view of the immense fortune aboard, do you believe there are any chances that a conspiracy of the crew or passengers has arisen?"

"I do not know," replied the first speaker. "The fortune in precious metals and gems points to that, but on the other hand, during the last three or four years there have been other mysterious disappearances of spacecraft, such as the *Antarian*."

"And the *Prestol*," added another of the four.

"Both of which were supposed to have gone out of control and to have been drawn into the sun."

"Presumably."

"Why do you say that?"

"Because, do you not think it rather queer, that is, beyond the possibility of coincidence, that every one of these missing craft should disappear without radioing one of the planets of their distress?"

"That is true."

"Of course, in these past disappearances there have been attempts to solve the mystery of how these space flyers all disappeared with dead radios—there is the flaw—but previously, all efforts have proved futile. This time, we must not give up until we know what has become of the *Interplanetary Limited.*"

"Isn't it possible that the *Limited* might have been destroyed by some large meteor? That would preclude the possibilities of its sending a radio message."

"If that is so, like the cases of the *Graphand* and the *Ustal,* which were destroyed by meteors through a failure of their repellor rays to function properly, we shall find wreckage of the ship somewhere. But in these past disappearances, no wreckage has been found."

"Suppose the crew or passengers had connived to rob the ship, where could they go? There would be no refuge for them on any of the three worlds."

"True enough."

"What are we to do?"

"Investigation is now under way. The telescopes are examining the route between Mars and Venus, while teams of astronauts are being sent out in their space flyers to find some trace of the missing ship. All we can do now is to wait for the result of the investigation."

*   *   *

Within the depths of the Earth's satellite, the five captives of the moon pirates awaited the hour of judgment. To their imaginations, their future was not to be a pleasant one. So for hours they waited in the oppressive silence of the gray somber tomb, until they should be called upon to hear their respective fates officially meted out to them, though they had already guessed what disposal to expect at the hands of the pirates. Sleep had overcome the girl, mercifully sparing her a few agonized hours of mortal suspense. The four men sat in dejected silence, intent upon their own personal retrospections, occasionally passing a word. The long hours rolled by, suddenly a vibration shook the floor, awakening the girl whose head lay pillowed in the lap of her father. She sat up with a start, her confused mind abruptly aroused from sleep, unable for the moment to fully reconstruct the series of events leading up to the present situation in which the five now found themselves.

"What was that, daddy?" she asked looking up into the grave, haggard countenance of her father.

"The floor's beginning to rise," replied Jan Trenton. "We are about to be released from this dungeon to see what Carconte has decided to do with us..."

Slowly the floor rose once more until it came upon a level with the doorway. As they had expected, several of the moon pirates were there to escort them into the presence of the pirate chief.

"Come," said one of the space brigands, "we await your reception into our council room."

The monotonous oratory of the man bespoke the fact that he had repeated this particular passage many times before. The man led the way, the five captives following. Behind them came three more of the moon pirates who brought up the rear of the procession. They traversed a series of corridors and halls, up stairways and around bends in the numerous passages in the labyrinth of the moon chambers, the four pirates finally bringing them to a stop before a pair of high, massive doors, which were closed.

The doors opened slightly, allowing a red, lurid glow to pass through the narrow crack, and then swinging aside noiselessly, the avenue was opened up before them. Complete silence reigned within the high domed chamber as the five captives were ushered within.

CHAPTER SEVEN
The Chamber of Moving Skeletons

A HORRIBLE sight met their eyes! Grouped about the sides of the chamber, sitting or else standing upon the elevated dais which encircled the long room, where as many as fifty or more human skeletons! In lifelike postures, they were arranged about the sides of the chamber, and the vacant, sightless skulls seemed as if focused upon the awe-stricken group of prisoners from the *Interplanetary Limited,* glaring at them menacingly! At the far end, upon a dais, a skeleton sat alone away from the rest, apparently the overlord of this grisly crew.

A vibrant scream shattered the oppressive silence, which hung like a dismal mantle of gloom over the death chamber with its sepulchral company. Again the piercing scream split the awful quietude of the horrid room, as the girl pointed with shaking finger at one of the skeletons!

"By all the suns of the Universe," exclaimed Sorelle, "it's moving!"

And in truth it was. The grim portender of death moved its skull slightly sideways, while a bony arm with claw-like hands reached for a cord and pulled it! A tinkling bell sounded, and heralded a startling effect. Every skeleton that was sitting down arose to its feet, while those, which had already assumed standing posture, turned their gaze from the prisoners to the solitary skeleton upon the raised dais at the room's end, the hollow sockets of the white skulls all directed upon this one skeleton. A shudder ran through the group of prisoners as the grinning jaws of a nearby member of the terrible crew opened and closed with a snapping click! What a terrible scene this was—one to shatter the nerves of the bravest with its uncanny potentialities...

"What makes them capable of movement?" whispered Quenden to Trenton.

"No conversation..." came the dismal admonishment of the lone skeleton at the far end of the room, pointing an accusing finger at the group.

To the young astronaut the voice sounded strangely familiar. Where had he heard it before? The skeleton's jaw commenced moving once more as it intoned the following announcement:

"You are in the Council Room of Death and will soon receive the judgment of the moon pirates..."

The five captives stared, fascinated at the grisly array of skeletons who had relaxed from their silence, and now sighs, coughs and whispers were heard from the ranks of the bony caricatures. Jan Trenton now recognized the voice; it was that of Carconte! He wondered how the pirate leader could speak through the medium of the skeleton so easily in synchronization with the movements of the thing, especially of the jaws.

The dull red hue of the room changed gradually to a blue color, and above the head of the lone skeleton there shone a full moon upon whose silvery surface lay silhouetted in black lines a skull and cross bones.

Scarcely had the red glow of the chamber resolved itself into a blue color, when a mysterious change began to creep over the skeletons! Dim, vague, shadowy outlines commenced to enshroud the bones and the grisly crew began to disappear from view, fading into something as yet intangible which was attempting to manifest itself. The dim shadows prevailed over the bony structures of the skeletons and before the wide distended eyes of the five prisoners there appeared the living bodies of the moon pirates, standing in the exact positions previously occupied by the skeletons!

Then the truth struck the little group suddenly as they realized that by a clever lighting system of mysterious powers, the flesh and clothing surrounding the skeletons of the moon pirates had been rendered invisible, producing the weird effect they had just witnessed.

The lone figure at the far end of the room was Carconte, whose face grinned in evil anticipation at them, while ranged around the sides of the room were the rest of the pirates. The aluminum-capped Hulan was not in sight.

"Before we announce our decision concerning the fate of you five, we have a few matters to which we shall attend first," said Carconte. "Take seats and look on."

The pirates who had escorted them to the council chamber, and who had stood behind them during the amazing scene and transition they had witnessed, now led them to a row of seats at the rear of the chamber.

"We have first of all a member of our ranks who is to meet punishment and death!" cried Carconte loudly. "He's a traitor who attempted to steal a large quantity of our gains and desert us. He was caught in the very act of transporting the booty from our treasure room to the space flyer in which he had intended reaching Mars! His perfidy, and subsequent fate, which you are about to see enacted before your eyes, will teach you all an object lesson. Following the terrible penalty we mete out to traitors, there is one within our ranks who has honestly strived to benefit our organization and who has succeeded in accomplishing his illustrious purpose. As a contrasting example, he shall be rewarded."

As if awaiting the termination of his speech, two sections of the floor slid aside, and up through the cavity within the center of the chamber there arose a platform containing two men and an array of intricate apparatus. It took but a single glance to recognize Nez Hulan, the human robot, who stood at the side of one of the machines. Fastened to a steel column by means of a metal girdle around his waist was a man none of the captives had ever seen before. Evidently he was the traitorous moon pirate.

"You are about to die!" spoke Carconte pointing a denunciatory finger at the abject figure of the moon pirate. He slumped forward in the iron girdle in melancholy resignation to his impending fate. "But before you die, the manner of your passing is to be exemplified in the presence of our entire organization, so that never shall there occur a repetition of your act. Hereafter, a member of our band will think twice before yielding to temptation. I now turn you over to Hulan who shall see that you receive fit punishment. What he has in store for you, I do not know, but that we shall all enjoy it, I am sure!"

"I shall first of all remove the man's sanity," rasped Hulan, his metal head and steel limbs glittering in the light. "Watch it go."

The cruel machine man placed a round metal cap down over the victim's head, and then directed the terminal of one of his machines toward the man. A strange flickering of dark shadows engulfed the platform on which the two men and scientific apparatus was placed, making the scene within the center of the council room appear like a shady vision of unreality. From out of the dark haze surrounding the apparatus there stood out in dim relief the pale countenance of Hulan with his cruel, merciless, supercilious smile. The shadowy form of the moon pirate could hardly be distinguished from the other objects until presently the flickering ceased, the dark haze dissipating itself into dissolution. The scene became clear before the interested eyes of some fifty or sixty moon pirates, as well as those of the five captives, who were gripped in a horrid, hypnotic fascination.

The form of the moon pirate writhed and squirmed, attempting to escape the confines of the girdle while, upon the lips of the unfortunate buccaneer, there arose an incoherent sound such as an animal might make, the torment of the man manifesting itself in the repugnant mouthings and terrible grimaces he made. Vainly he tried to free himself of the retaining girdle that bound him to the steel shaft, his arms clawing futilely at its encircling embrace. Hulan looked on in amused contempt. The man with the rubber heart directed a tiny, fine needle-point ray of light upon the luckless moon pirate, and now the man's attempts to release himself from the steel girdle were frantic, while his raving rose to a dismal howl of mingled pain, terror, and anguish.

The five prisoners shut their eyes against the disgusting sight. But they could not shut out the unearthly sounds made by the maniac. Presently the sounds of the man were silenced, and when they looked again it was to see the drooping form of the moon pirate bent forward in lifeless attitude.

"Is he dead?" asked Clarkford in a low whisper, unable to maintain his silence any longer.

"I don't know," replied Trenton. "That devilish ray did something to him!"

"It's horrible!" shuddered the girl. "What beasts they are!"

"He isn't dead yet!" exclaimed Sorelle. "Look—he's moving..."

The tortured man stirred vaguely, and passed a hand over his forehead.

Hulan spoke again, "The man's sanity has been satisfactorily removed, I shall now illustrate to you what would happen if your bones should suddenly soften and become liquid."

The mechanical-limbed man turned to a machine that arose above his head, and directed its luminous, ghostly rays upon the body of the doomed man who had lapsed into a stupor. Nothing happened until the light faded away, and then a perceptible, restless movement of the man's body became noticeable.

"The rays of light that are now turned upon the subject," stated the hard, cold voice of the aluminum headed wizard, "are invisible to your eyes due to the fact that their vibrations are of such high periodicity as to be beyond the reach of optical perception. I first discovered their powers when I experimented upon Professor Cimm at Fomar. He was unaware of the experiment until it was all over, and then he never knew what had happened to him."

The body no longer stirred. Was he dead? Hulan's next act answered that question which was now predominant in the minds of all those who were watching.

"He appears to be dead, but he isn't. His mentality has been destroyed and the dissolution of his bones has rendered him incapable of any articulation—also of movement to a certain extent—but watch!"

Again the tiny finger of light played over the moon pirate whose treachery had met this fate. Wherever the ray of light settled, there arose a quivering.

"This tiny light is the most excellent medium of torture ever invented by man," said Hulan. "Seven hundred years ago such pirates as Morgan, Kidd, L'Ollonais, and Lafitte believed themselves to be proficient in the art of torture, but their results were mere child's play beside those brought about by this tiny finger of light. Even the ancient inquisition with its alleged horrors, are as nothing compared to what you have witnessed! I have even surpassed the dreaded Durna Rangue cult, which sprang up and died upon Mars over a hundred years ago when the earthly colonies to that planet were young and the cult fled the Earth to escape prosecution.

"And now for the final act!"

The arch demon, half man and half machine, who had lain dead and mutilated within the depths of space, now picked up a long rod whose end terminated in a broad, hollow snout.

The pirate mastermind turned the terrible ray of yellow light upon what was left of the moon pirate who had essayed to desert the ranks of the lunar buccaneers, taking with him a large share of treasure. The remains of the body rapidly disappeared. Where the man had previously stood there now existed nothing.

"Let that be a lesson!" warned Carconte, who had been greatly impressed by the display of inhuman cruelty derived from the perverted intellect of Nez Hulan.

The five captives were a bit unnerved by the insidious spectacle they had been forced to watch. Centuries before, on the seas of the Earth, there had been pirates who robbed, killed, and tortured; but in cruelty they did not compare with the moon pirates.

"Take your apparatus away, Hulan," ordered Carconte. "We have now to bestow upon the head of a true comrade the reward of a special service to us."

Slowly the platform sank beneath the floor once more, bearing the cruel, pale, countenanced Hulan and his weird, devilish contrivances out of sight. Just before his head disappeared below the floor level, the group of five shuddered as they met his sneering gaze eyeing them malevolently. The floor closed together above the cavity into which the platform had descended.

"Portho Zind!" announced Carconte in a loud voice.

The man, known previously to the passengers of the *Interplanetary Limited* as Balfour, stepped forward from the sidelines of the pirates, and faced his superior.

"As a reward for your information from Deliphon in regards to the *Interplanetary Limited*, which we have captured, you are to be elevated in position among us, and your quarter moon is to be replaced by the full moon itself," said Carconte.

There ensued a repetition of the occurrence that had taken place upon the *Jolly Roger* when Brentley and his two comrades had received the crescents of the moon pirates, except that this time it was Zind who had a full moon indelibly stamped over that of the quarter moon. There existed but one symbol higher than the full moon, and that was a full moon surrounded by a red circle. Only two of the pirates boasted these. Carconte wore one on his right forearm, while Hulan, who had no arm through which to implant the moon's outline along with its skull and cross bones, had the insignia of the moon pirates upon his chest, just above the spot where a long white scar marked the removal of the punctured heart. The group of five prisoners from the *Interplanetary Limited* paid little attention to the proceedings, being absorbed in the contemplation of their own impending fates, which were soon to be discussed.

Zind received his full moon, the height of recognition in the ranks of the moon pirates, which would accord him a marked preference over his brothers who bore only the crescent or quarter moon, and assured him a larger share of the spoils and booty that fell in their way.

"And now," said Carconte, as if in afterthought, "we have with us five guests who I hope have enjoyed our little entertainment. Three of them are to become members of our band, I hope, and our friend Hulan wishes the fourth one for his experiments. Doubtless he may wish to put on another little show of some kind like the one we witnessed just now. The woman is to be mine!"

With the last words, Carconte stood at full height, folded his arms across his chest, and with bald head gleaming in the light of the chamber, paused emphatically. Sorelle appeared the least perturbed of the group. Upon the face of Jan Trenton there lay a look of intense hatred as he eyed the arrogant pirate chieftain, his fingers clenching and unclenching, eager to be at the throat of the pirate leader. Clarkford's face reflected both anger and terror, for he had not forgotten the outlines of the experiments that Hulan had explained to Professor Crayton. Crayton was to have been the one experimented upon. Now that Crayton had gone and committed suicide, it would be Clarkford. Quenden's face bore a desperate look that had been born of both loathing and anger at the scene he had witnessed, for it was *farthest* from his desires to go under the knife at the hands of Hulan, and he would take the same stand as Trenton in his refusal to join the moon pirates as Bentley and his two companions had taken.

"Are you three men ready to become moon pirates?" queried Carconte of Trenton, Sorelle, and Quenden.

"No," replied Quenden.

"Never," was the ultimatum of Jan Trenton.

"When hell freezes over!" was Sorelle's promise.

"I see that Hulan has a little work to do on you men before you are willing," said Carconte, disregarding the stinging insult Sorelle had applied to the villainous crowd. "It would be more sensible to yield now, for I cannot promise that Hulan will make the operation painless, and if anything should happen that the *experiment* failed, it would mean the disintegrator gun, and a ride into space, or else death under the disintegrator beams.

The three men remained silent.

"And what do you say to becoming the woman of Carconte, my pretty one?" queried the pirate leader, attempting a coquettish gesture, which made him appear the more hideous.

"I much prefer the disintegrator gun!" replied the girl, "but if you will spare my father and these other brave men, letting them go, I shall yield to you willingly."

"Oh, will you?" smirked the evil Carconte, evidently stung by the girl's words, which had upset his pride and dignity in the presence of his men. "And suppose you don't come willingly—what then? Merely this—Carconte will have the pleasure of breaking you to his will, and shall give to your father and his three companions horrible deaths, slow, painful, drawn out hours of agonized torture! Hulan will be delighted; he never tires of such sport!"

The girl broke down and sobbed, her father and the young astronaut springing forward simultaneously to support her swaying form and comfort her. The whole effort upon the girl's part to save her father from the terrors of the experiment, and to release the others from becoming moon pirates at the hands of Hulan, had amounted to naught.

"Let your four companions go?" mimicked the pirate leader. "So that they could bring a swarm of spacecraft down about our heads from the three worlds? Do you think I am a fool?"

"I know you are," said Clarkford bitingly, "to even think that any one of us would allow my daughter to desecrate herself by voluntarily becoming a pawn for our freedom!"

"I'll give you your reply when Hulan has your head cut off from that mangy body of yours," retorted Carconte angrily.

"You'll still be able to hear and understand what I am saying!"

"You can draw and quarter me if you wish, but spare my daughter," pleaded Clarkford, tears moistening his eyes. "I have given you my bonds, and offered you my life. What else is there to take?"

"Nothing!" rasped an unpleasant voice in the rear of the group. "Nothing that we cannot take if it is our wish…"

Turning at sound of the voice, the five prisoners gazed into the face of Hulan, the human robot, whose steel arm pointed like the finger of doom at Clarkford.

"You will not be drawn and quartered," said the machine man in icy tones. "I have other plans for you, and I do not want your life. I want your body. You will not be killed, though before we are through, you shall beg for somebody to kill you…"

The blood of the five captives ran cold with the horror of Hulan's veiled suggestions.

"You merciless villain!" swore Clarkford vehemently, realizing that all the threats, promises and entreaties in three worlds would not change the intentions of this man of blood and iron.

"Come," said Hulan, placing a steel hand heavily upon the shoulder of the condemned man, "you are mine—part of my share of the spoils from the *Limited*. I have you; Carconte has your daughter, although if I had her she would die, for women are trouble to such as we, the other three men go to the pirate crew, and everyone is satisfied as far as our hostages are concerned. Get along with you…fast!"

Hulan's steel fingers bit into the shoulder of Clarkford so hard that the condemned man nearly screamed with pain, and then his daughter was upon the mechanical man, clawing and kicking him with the fury of a tigress. An annoyed look spread across Hulan's face, and with the other arm, he reached forward and clutched her white neck in a grip of steel that threatened to sever her jugular vein.

This was the signal for an infuriated young astronaut to hurl himself upon the metal-limbed moon pirate, and with a well directed blow, smash the scientific mastermind in the face so hard that he lost his hold upon the two captives and stumbled backward. In a cold fury of unreasoning hate, he caught Jan Trenton in a vise-like embrace with his steel arms, and would have crushed the ribs of the young astronaut had not Quenden and Sorelle sprang forward to his assistance. By this time, the moon pirates were pouring from their stations along the side of the chamber and were milling about the combatants, striving to separate them.

Above the noise of the melee there roared the voice of Carconte, yelling and threatening for order.

"Stop!" he commanded in a loud voice. "Get back to your positions!"

Angrily, the pirate chief strode down the length of the council chamber as his men hurried discreetly back to their places once more in compliance with his order. With furious mien he confronted Hulan.

"Leave your dirty, iron fingers off my woman!" he roared, pointing at the black marks which were beginning to appear upon the neck of Suzette. "If you harm her, I'll break every cog and wheel in those legs and arms of yours, and have that rubber heart out of you in the bargain! Take your man, but don't touch any of the others; they are not yours."

Hulan did as he was bid, humbly accepting the abuse in silence. Though Hulan was by far the intellectual superior of Carconte and the rest of the pirates, being the mastermind of them all, he lacked the leadership and backbone that made Carconte the pirate chieftain. Hulan was at heart a coward. The men all feared him, and looked upon him with awe, but they never held the respect for him that they did for

Carconte, and had it not been for their leader, Hulan would have met his doom long before this.

"Take these men away," ordered Carconte to several of the moon pirates. "Our meeting is over. Leave the woman here—she is mine, and I shall attend to her later…"

As Hulan disappeared with Clarkford, he mumbled something under his breath, a cold hard look mantling his deathly white features. Had anyone been close enough to have overheard his muttered comment, they would have gathered enough from his words to understand that already the woman had made trouble among them.

"Tomorrow," promised the pirate leader, addressing the three men, "you will be interviewed again, and if your answer is still the same, it will be necessary for Hulan to operate upon your brains."

As they were escorted out of the council chamber, Jan Trenton cast a last look upon Suzette Clarkford, a look in which there was a world of meaning, and in his eyes were the parting instructions which her mind intuitively guessed: that she was not to forget the radium pill he had given to her, but to forbear using it until the final moment, when it seemed that the last vestige of hope had dwindled away.

"Hurry along!" snapped the pirate behind the young astronaut, giving him a shove through the great doorway leading into the council chamber.

CHAPTER EIGHT
"I'll get Hulan for You!"

ONCE more the three men were led through the maze of corridors and rooms that constituted the underground chambers of the moon pirates. This time they were led to more spacious quarters consisting of not only one room but several, and upon entering they immediately fell to exploring them while they discussed their situation.

"It looks as if we are here to stay," remarked Sorelle.

"We have until tomorrow to decide," said Quenden, "and as far as I can see we are going to be moon pirates eventually either way we decide.

"They'll have to operate upon my brain, and remove my conscience first of all," stated Jan Trenton.

"I sure would hate to be Clarkford now," spoke Quenden, shaking his head ruefully. "Hulan seemed eager to get his hands on him and to begin the experiment."

"Not much worse than the fate of the girl," observed Sorelle.

"There is an escape for her," said the young astronaut.

"An escape—what do you mean?"

"Death."

"Death?"

"Yes."

"How?"

Then the pilot of the *Interplanetary Limited* explained how he had given the fatal radium pill to the girl.

"Too bad you didn't have one for her father," observed Sorelle. "He would have appreciated it."

"Perhaps he shall have such an opportunity as was offered Crayton," suggested Quenden cryptically.

"I doubt it," said Trenton. "Hulan will be watching him close to see that he doesn't lose another subject by suicide."

"Not bad quarters, eh?" remarked Sorelle, taking in the four chambers of their elaborate prison with a wave of his hand.

The four rooms were furnished with comfortable lounges and expensive fittings as well as numerous conveniences—and luxuries that the three men were surprised to find in this subterranean recluse of the moon pirates.

"They pilfered all this from the spaceships that they captured," said the astronaut as the three men walked through the four rooms for a closer examination. Their initial investigation had been more or less cursory.

"No chance for escape here," said Quenden. "The door's closed behind us by means of a great sheet of metal, which slides down from above the doorway, and evidently the last room is a blind alley because there are no more doors opening out from it."

A grating noise came from behind them.

"They're raising the door," observed Sorelle.

"And closing it again," added Trenton as with a rattling sound the door slid back into place.

The three captives hurried into the main room. There upon the floor just inside the door was a large quantity of food.

"They're not going to starve us, anyway," commented Sorelle as he fell to eating.

The three were hungry, though in the excitement of the preceding events they had not been aware of it, and soon they had cleared up the victuals brought them by the moon pirates.

"You don't suppose Hulan has put any poison in this food we have eaten do you?" asked Quenden.

"A fine time to bring that up," remarked Sorelle, eyeing Quenden critically.

"Well, I didn't want to spoil your appetite."

"If they were bent on killing us, Hulan would insist upon a more scientifically cruel manner," said Trenton.

"I'm sleepy," yawned Sorelle.

"So am I," said Quenden.

"We might as well sleep," advised Sorelle. "No one knows but what we shall need all the rest we can get before this affair is through."

Quenden and Bret Sorelle curled up in comfortable positions on the lounges and soon were in deep sleep. Jan Trenton was sleepless. He sat lost in gloomy meditation regarding the fate that had fallen to the lot of the five prisoners. He was especially worried over Suzette Clarkford. Carconte had taken her. What had happened? Had she been forced to swallow the radium pill yet? If so, she must be dead. He wondered. For several long hours he sat there.

He became restless and tired of sitting in one spot. The astronaut wished he might get some sleep, and envied his two companions, but his troubled mind would not allow him to sleep. He arose and walked about the four chambers, examining the contents of the rooms. A draped hanging upon the wall close to the ceiling piqued his curiosity and he stood upon a large chair to examine it, leaning his hand against the wall. As he did so, a large section of the wall yawned open before him. That portion beneath his hand sank backward so rapidly that he lost his balance upon the chair and tumbled to the floor with a crash, overturning the ponderous piece of furniture.

Sitting upon the floor where he had fallen, Jan Trenton gazed mystified at the wall where the stone-work had given way before him. The opening was no longer there; only the blank wall stared back at him. Once more the young astronaut climbed upon the chair, and gingerly pressed upon the same spot in the wall he had previously leaned against.

Slowly, the section of wall, large enough for a man to enter, swung aside, disclosing to the eager eyes of the astronaut a secret tunnel. The astronaut put a foot inside, and then hesitated. Should he enter without notifying his two fellow prisoners? What unknown perils lay before him—suppose he should not return, and they should awake to find him gone? Gradually he came to reconsider his intentions, and withdrew his foot and hand, allowing the wall to swing back into place once more.

Going back into first of the four rooms, he awakened Sorelle and Quenden.

"Are they here for us?" asked Quenden, sitting up suddenly as Trenton shook him, after having brought Sorelle to his senses.

"Come, you two. I've just found something I want to show you..." exclaimed the young astronaut excitedly.

Together, the three men hurried to the fourth and last room of their apartments to where the astronaut had discovered the secret tunnel. Standing upon the chair, Trenton depressed the section of wall, which slid silently backward to reveal the opening of the concealed passage.

"A secret room!" gasped Sorelle.

"No...a tunnel," corrected Jan Trenton who was craning his neck to see farther within the dimly lit confines of the secret annex to their apartment.

"Where does it lead?" asked Quenden.

"That's what we're going to find out..." said Trenton.

"No sooner said than done!" exclaimed Sorelle in whom immediate action was characteristic.

"Wait!" remonstrated the young astronaut. "Shall we all go?"

"Why not?" asked Sorelle.

"Suppose the moon pirates find us gone?"

"All the better," chuckled the adventurer. "It will give them something to scratch their heads over!"

"Good. Let's go!"

The three men hastily piled into the narrow tunnel, the wall swinging back into place behind them. Cautiously they made their way along the passage, wondering where it led.

"Do you notice how thick and undisturbed the dust is where it has settled?" queried Jan Trenton in a whisper.

"Yes," replied Quenden. "It gets into my nose, and it's all I can do to keep from sneezing."

"Do you know what that means?" asked Trenton.

"What? My sneezing or the dust?" asked Quenden.

"The dust," replied the astronaut. "It suggests the fact that the moon pirates are unaware of this hidden passage's existence. They won't know where to look for us! This layer of dust is the accumulation of many years, and it has lain here undisturbed, which perpetuates the fact that the moon pirates have never come into this secret tunnel."

"Then we have escaped from them!" exclaimed Quenden.

"For the time being," replied Trenton.

"Let's see where it will take us," said Sorelle, leading the way onward through the passage whose rocky floor lay coated with the dust.

Finally, the three men reached the end of the long tunnel, which it would seem had led them several hundred feet away from their prison quarters.

"Another secret door!" echoed Sorelle in a hoarse whisper, as he pointed to the extremity of the tunnel.

"Shhh!" remonstrated Trenton, holding up a finger to his lips for silence. "I hear voices…"

And sure enough, from beyond the secret wall panel there came the sound of voices in conversation. The three prisoners leaned up against the panel, and listened eagerly.

"It's some of the pirates," whispered Sorelle as he caught the gist of their conversation.

"What are they talking about?" asked Quenden.

"I can't quite make out," replied Bret Sorelle, "but from the sound of the voices I should say there were three or four of them in there."

Presently the voices died down and dwindled away.

"They have gone," said Quenden.

"Let's go in," suggested Trenton.

"Sure," replied Sorelle. "If you think it's safe to take a chance."

"We'll try it," said the young astronaut as he pulled upon the paneling that separated the secret tunnel and the next room.

"Go carefully," admonished Quenden.

Slowly, Jan Trenton drew the section of wall inward and the three gazed into the room, temporarily devoid of human presence.

"Look!" directed the astronaut, his eyes glistening as he pointed out to his companions several objects that lay upon the table in the room.

"Atom pistols!" Sorelle exclaimed softly.

With a light, catlike bound, Jan Trenton leaped down from the opening and was followed by Sorelle and Quenden, the three captives seizing the coveted weapons.

"Now I feel better!" said Trenton.

"A-ha!" grinned Sorelle as he clutched one of the guns in his right hand. "This is more like it. Now maybe we'll have something to say about whether or not we become moon pirates!"

All three were delighted at their good fortune and did not notice the sound of approaching footsteps, until there appeared in the doorway leading from the chamber one of the moon pirates whose startled eyes took in the scene before him. His hands leaped to the atom pistol at his side, but Quenden, who was the first to see him, beat him to the draw, already having the pistol in his hand, and with a muffled gasp the pirate sank to the floor.

"That's for Bronson!" said Quenden, mentioning the name of one of his dead comrades who had been shot from the large atom gun aboard the *Jolly Roger.* "We've got one of the scoundrels to our credit, anyway!"

"We have one desperate chance in our power!" exclaimed the young astronaut excitedly. "We must fight our way to a broadcaster, and radio Earth for help!"

"Good enough!" agreed Sorelle, enthusiastically. "It's our one chance, and we must lose no time…"

With atom guns clutched firmly in their hands, the three desperate men proceeded stealthily along the corridor leading from the room they had just quitted.

"Wait a minute," said Trenton. "We had better put that fellow you just killed out of sight. More can be accomplished by strategy than by a show of arms."

"Put him in the secret tunnel," suggested Quenden.

The three hastily reentered the room, and taking the body of the moon pirate, they placed it just inside the secret passage and closed the door.

"That takes care of him," said the young astronaut as the three proceeded on their way once more.

"Have you any idea where we're going?" queried Sorelle.

"No," replied Trenton. "We'll just have to trust to luck."

From the bend ahead, they heard footsteps approaching.

"The pirates!" exclaimed Sorelle in a hoarse whisper. "Shall we drill them?"

"There's too many from the sound," said Trenton. "We had better hide and let them go past, or the noise will bring the whole crowd down around our ears!"

"In here!" hissed Quenden, motioning them to a small room leading off the corridor. "Quick!"

They ducked out of sight just in time before several of the pirates appeared around the bend. Hulan the human robot was among them.

"A close shave…" commented Sorelle.

"Or a gun duel!" added Trenton. "I wish I knew where their broadcaster was. They must have one somewhere nearby."

The three members of the *Interplanetary Limited* continued their way, turning the bend in the passage, and heading rapidly for a room at the far end. On tiptoe, they approached the doorway of the chamber, and soon they heard voices.

"Well, how do you feel now?" spoke a smooth, oily voice which tickled their memory with its peculiar enunciation. "You must admit that Hulan is a genius."

"He's a devil," came the weak reply. "Oh, put me out of my misery. I implore you…"

Then followed a groan of pain and anguish as only the damned in hell might emit, followed by a harsh, wicked laugh.

"Kill me! Kill me!" continued the weak voice in pleading accents.

"Clarkford!" exclaimed Trenton as he heard the tortured accents of the man for the second time.

"And the other one sounds like Balfour," said Quenden.

"You mean Zind!" corrected Sorelle. "There's no one else in there from what I can hear—let's rescue Clarkford!"

The three broke into the room, atom pistols ready for immediate use.

Confronting them was the most horrible scene they had ever witnessed, or would ever be called upon to see, a scene that was to be stamped vividly upon their memory in graphic detail for the remainder of their lives!

Unwittingly they had stumbled upon the laboratory of Nez Hulan, and before their eyes lay a most terrible, unnerving spectacle of such hideous character as civilized man is seldom called upon to witness. Upon a supporting standard above a complicated array of attached tubes, wires, and other intricate apparatus the decapitated head of J. C. Clarkford rested! An expression of intense pain and horror lay upon his countenance! A short distance from the head, across the room and facing it, was the body of the man whose arms and legs still moved at the commands of the brain, which was hooked up in communication with the head by the system of tubes and wires that ran from the apparatus surrounding the head to the various portions of the body!

Standing before the gruesome handiwork of the inhuman genius of Hulan, stood Zind, apparently enjoying the horrifying scene. The dark-skinned pirate turned from his pleasure of taunting the head as he heard the entrance of the three men from the *Interplanetary Limited* who had been taken captives by the murderous crew, an ugly scowl spreading over his features at the sight of them. The horror of the thing struck Trenton, Sorelle, and Quenden dumb for the brief moment in which Zind was overcome by their sudden, unexpected appearance. Even the head stared in surprise.

"What are you doing here?" growled Zind, his dark face glaring in evil hatred at them as his hand slowly crept to the suspicious bulge of a gun butt at his side.

"Take your hand away from that atom pistol or you'll never know!" snapped the astronaut, covering the olive skinned spy of the moon pirates with the menacing muzzle of his gun. "Now tell us where there is a broadcaster, or we'll shoot you so full of holes you can pass for the proverbial Swiss cheese of yore…"

"You'll die for this!" hissed Zind, his lips curling in a sneer. "A long, slow death under the tiny ray!"

"Shut up, you dirty dog," came the sharp command from Sorelle, who approached and shoved his weapon against the man's ribs. "If we do die that way, you won't be there to see us go. Now speak up and tell us where that broadcaster is located, or it is death for you!"

"Oh, kill me! Put me out of my agony! Save my daughter!" whispered the head, faintly. "You, Trenton, will do it for me, won't you? Shoot me, quick, in the head…destroy my body…"

"How long have you been like this?" asked the young astronaut, addressing the head.

"When Hulan got me here, I lost my senses; when I came to an hour ago I found myself as you see me—looking across the room at my own body! It isn't the pain so much; it's some terrible feeling I can't explain—it's unworldly, like something never before experienced in human ken. It's a terrible sensation. I must die! I must! It's seizing me—it's on my head. If you ever valued my friendship, kill me, Trenton! It's the most merciful thing you can do."

The three men, forgetting Zind for a moment, stared aghast at the words uttered through the lips of Clarkford's head, which had apparently been severed at the junction of the neck and chest.

"Watch out, Sorelle!" yelled Quenden snapping his gun into position and firing from the hip. Zind, in the space of the few seconds in which the attention of the three had been diverted to the decapitated man, had raised a large, heavy instrument above the head of the adventurer.

A silent, blue streak spit from the muzzle of Quenden's atom gun, and for the second time since their escape, the sniping prowess of the man claimed the life of a moon pirate.

"That's for Brekstadt!" announced Quenden coolly, naming the second member of the *Limited's* crew who had been consigned to the huge atom gun aboard the *Jolly Roger.*

"The radio, you say?" queried Clarkford weakly, while the hands of the decapitated body stirred in a characteristic gesture of query. "It's in the private quarters of Carconte—I heard Hulan say so. My daughter is there—save her! Kill me—that awful feeling—it isn't pain—it's indescribable!"

There followed a groan from between the lips, and the body of the man writhed in an attempt to get away from something.

"We'll have to do it," announced Sorelle to his two reluctant comrades. "It's the only thing to be done. He can't be saved. We must act before Hulan comes back with the rest of the gang, too!"

"It's horrible—but I guess it's necessary," agreed Trenton.

"Yes, kill me..." implored the head of Clarkford. "Please don't leave me to suffer like this. Don't leave my body intact for that beast to work on, either. Destroy it!"

"Goodbye, Clarkford..." spoke Sorelle in a choking voice.

"I'll get Hulan for you!" swore the avenging Quenden.

"And if your daughter isn't dead, I'll save her," promised Jan Trenton. "Carconte shall die!"

"Farewell..." smiled Clarkford, as he saw the pistols of the three slowly and reluctantly raised to point at his head. "I'll meet you all some time in another existence beyond the plane of the three worlds!"

With a simultaneous succession of blue flashes from each of the three guns, the decapitated head of Clarkford disappeared from view, leaving but a few fragmentary remains. The three men turned their attention to the body which was likewise riddled beyond practical use for experiment in the laboratory.

CHAPTER NINE
The Duel to Death

"WHERE now?" asked Quenden after the loathsome business had been completed.

"To the apartment of Carconte, and death to every miserable pirate who shows his face!" announced Jan Trenton.

"Where are Carconte's rooms?" asked Sorelle.

"That's something we must find out," said Trenton. "Come on!"

The three passed out of the laboratory of Nez Hulan and into the passage once more. Cautioning his two comrades with a remonstrating gesture for silence, the astronaut sneaked ahead of them along the corridor with the stealth of a cat. Sorelle and Quenden were perplexed for a moment at this strange maneuver, until ahead of them they saw a moon pirate who, with back toward them, was busily engaged in some item of work or preoccupation. The first he knew of their presence was when a pair of strong fingers closed over his throat, choking off the cry which instinctively issued from his lungs. Turned roughly about, the moon buccaneer's startled gaze rested upon Jan Trenton.

"One peep out of you, and I'll wring your neck off!" threatened the astronaut.

"A dose of the pistol for you too, if you don't tell us where Carconte's rooms are located," added Sorelle who had come up beside the two, poking his atom gun against the head of the frightened moon pirate significantly.

"There—that way!" directed the buccaneer, his bulging eyes rolling fearfully in the direction of the menacing pistol whose cold muzzle rested against his temple.

"Lead us there," ordered Trenton.

The man's obedient efforts to comply with their wishes were ludicrous. Evidently life was precious to the rascal. He led them along the corridor in the direction of his chieftain's quarters, even admonishing them to be silent. The boring muzzle of Sorelle's gun carried a great deal of persuasion and left no doubt within the mind of the lunar buccaneer as to what he should do. Down the corridor and through several rooms the moon pirate led them, finally showing a doorway down a low hall.

"There are Carconte's rooms, and the woman you seek is doubtless there, too," stated the pirate.

"Well...go on," said Sorelle.

"No—I'd much prefer you to kill me than to be ushered into the presence of Carconte. You saw what happened to the traitor whom Hulan tortured to death in the council chamber? That would be my fate were I to be found leading you here!"

"But you have no other choice," agreed Sorelle, tapping the pistol suggestively. "Carconte would realize that."

"Death is my other choice," replied the pirate, who, though terror stricken at the fate that awaited him should Sorelle's fingers close upon the knob of the gun, preferred such an end to the horrible death awaiting him at the hands of Nez Hulan.

"I can aid you no further," he maintained obstinately. "You must continue alone."

"While you sound the alarm," countered Trenton.

"No—I promise!" replied the pirate. "To do so would reveal the fact that I had brought you this far, and even my calling to arms the rest of my comrades might not exonerate me before the eyes of Hulan and Carconte—and they, as you already know, are not men to be trifled with…"

"Let him go," said Sorelle. "Even if I don't trust him, his logic is sound enough—and besides he would only be an encumbrance upon our hands. We'll have to chance it…"

"Skip!" ordered Trenton to the moon pirate, who hastily complied with the curt request, disappearing from sight around the bend in the corridor.

"Hurry up!" urged the young astronaut. "After all, we can't tell what the man may do!"

They pressed on towards the apartment of the pirate leader, and outside the doorway to the first room, they listened for voices. They heard none, and peering around the doorway Trenton perceived that the room was deserted.

"Come on—the way is clear!"

His two companions followed him through the room, and into the next.

"Where are the girl and the broadcaster?" queried Sorelle.

"That villain deceived us!" exclaimed Quenden vehemently. "He's probably bringing the rest of them here to annihilate us by now."

"Where do you sup—"

The words of Trenton were cut short by the piercing scream of a woman, coming from the direction of the doorway leading farther into the apartments of Carconte.

Without a moment's hesitation, the three raced swiftly through a succession of luxuriously furnished rooms, examining each one with a cursory, searching glance before proceeding to the next. Ahead of them they heard the sounds of a struggle, and to their ears came the deep vulgar tones of Carconte.

"You vixen—you miserable wench! So you would try to cheat me by destroying yourself? Well, you can't do it now because I took that poison away from you, even though I nearly twisted your pretty arm off to do it! Just for that, I'll take you to see your father! I was going to spare you the sight, but now you will be forced to look! Hulan has him ready to receive company!"

A coarse, vibrant laugh followed the last remark of Carconte, and then the three men of the spaceship *Limited* broke into the room, cutting short the laugh of the bald headed pirate who held the fainting girl by the wrist. Surprise, anger and hate mantled his face as he saw who the three men were. Nor did he wait for explanation but leaped across the room to where his atom gun lay upon the table.

The pistol of Sorelle silently spat fire, and with a terrible curse, which wrinkled his villainous face in a hideous grimace, he shook his left arm, which dangled limply from the effects of Sorelle's shot. Staggering up against the wall, the pirate chief pressed a button, and from the ceiling to the floor, dividing the room in half, there shot a close set formation of the deep, violet shafts of light that had barred the doorway of their cell upon the pirate spacecraft. Upon one side, stood Carconte, holding his injured arm, the fainting girl at his elbow, while upon the other side of the deadly screen stood the astronaut, adventurer and crew member of the *Interplanetary Limited.*

"Don't walk through that!" shrilled Quenden warningly. "Remember what happened to Crayton!"

Trenton's eyes blazed furiously and his atom pistol streaked forth its blue flashes in rapid succession at the leering pirate who stood behind the curtain of deadly, transparent rays. In spite of the pain in his arm, Carconte could not repress a guffaw of laughter as the astronaut fired shot after shot futilely at him through the curtain of violet light, which nullified the destroying forces of the atom gun.

"It's no use firing at him!" advised Sorelle. "We must find another way of getting across to that other side of the room."

"If I can't get over there," said Quenden, "I know what can!"

Quickly, he raised a heavy chair and balancing it upon his shoulders cast it across the room through the veil of deadly rays at the pirate chief who was running for a doorway leading from his side of the chamber! The chair caught him on the side of the head and down he crashed to the floor!

"Good!" ejaculated Sorelle. "But that doesn't help us in getting across there!"

"Watch!" directed Quenden, a sparkle of anticipation in his eye as he picked up another piece of furniture.

Straight for the other wall he threw it; right through the curtain of death it went, following the route of the chair, and smashing against the knob on the wall. The shaft of violet light disappeared, and, the three rushed across the room.

Trenton lifting Suzette Clarkford tenderly in his arms. She was beginning to recover her consciousness.

"We must get out of here!" cried Sorelle. "I hear the pirates coming!"

And indeed they were coming, a rush of many footsteps approaching the room in which stood the three men and the girl.

"We must get to the radio!" whispered Trenton.

"It's in one of the rooms we passed through!" exclaimed Quenden excitedly, motioning for them to follow him. "I saw it when we were coming here!"

Trenton, bearing the girl in his arms, followed Quenden, while Sorelle brought up the rear, guarding them from an attack in that direction.

"We'll hold them off while you are using the broadcaster," said Sorelle to Jan Trenton.

To the room in which Quenden had seen the broadcaster they continued, the running footsteps and excited yells and cries of the moon pirates growing rapidly louder.

*　　*　　*

Into the council chamber where the four men sat in conference at New York City, the, greatest metropolis on three worlds, there burst an excited man.

"The *Limited* has been captured and destroyed by the moon pirates!" shouted the man breathlessly.

"The moon pirates? Who are they?" questioned one of the officials blankly surprised.

"Thieves…space robbers!" exclaimed the man excitedly. They have captured the *Limited,* destroyed it, taken the treasure, killed part of the crew and its passengers, and the rest of them are in captivity upon the moon. At this moment they are fighting for their lives!"

"How do you know this?"

"They just radioed from the moon, having escaped from the moon pirates long enough to send the message for help."

"We must send them assistance immediately!"

"A swarm of fighting spacecraft is already on its way to the moon, having started ten minutes ago," announced the informant. "They should be half way there by now…"

"Moon pirates!" echoed the head official. "Can it be possible?"

"It explains the strange disappearance of all the spacecraft within the last few years."

"I remember reading of pirates in the olden days, way back in the past, several centuries ago, but these roved the seas of Earth to loot and murder among the sailing vessels."

"While nowadays the moon pirates cruise the seas of space to rob and destroy space flyers."

"How could they have existed upon the moon so long, without having been discovered? It seems that the information should have leaked out some way."

"Discipline and strict secrecy," explained one of the officials. "And they probably have a clever mastermind at the head of the group. I wonder how many their ranks number…?"

"Who sent the broadcast?" queried one of the officials, "and from what section of the moon did it come?"

"Jan Trenton stood before the broadcaster," said the man, "and behind him stood two men and a girl. A pale haggard look rested upon her face, and they were all excited and disheveled," replied the man. "I was at the receiving room when the flash came from the moon. I've forgotten the exact spot they gave. It was somewhere on the other side of the moon, and they scarcely knew themselves, and were able to give only an approximate estimate of their location."

"Jan Trenton!" exclaimed the official. "You probably all remember him and his narrow escape from death on Mars, when his space flyer became caught on the side of a meteor which plunged headlong toward the Martian planet."

"Yes, it seems that the meteor closely resembled a death's head."

"The Death's Head Meteor they called it."

"So there were four survivors—one of them a woman."

"Probably J. C. Clarkford's daughter."

"Let's hope the rescue ships arrive in time."

"In the meanwhile let's tune in on one of the fighting craft. We can obtain an accurate broadcast of the events as they transpire."

*　　*　　*

At the door of the broadcasting room, within range of the television screen, stood Quenden and Sorelle guarding against an overwhelming invasion of moon pirates, while the astronaut delivered his message to Earth, rotating nearly a quarter million miles away in space. From out of the bowels of the dead satellite across the cosmic void to the largest of the three planets the voice of Jan Trenton rang clear to throw into furor, excitement, and concern the population of a world, the news to be later relayed to Venus and Mars.

The guns of the two who were guarding the door spit silently as the vanguard of the moon pirates came into view. They had discovered their fallen leader who had been stunned from the blow delivered him by the chair. Quenden had hurled it with marked success. Before they could check their advance and make a retreat, two of the pirates had given up their lives to the marksmanship of Sorelle and Quenden. And then the moon pirates craftily betook themselves to advantageous positions where they could fire at the little group with the maximum safety to themselves.

"Hurry up with that broadcast!" urged Sorelle. "We can't hold them off much longer! The devils are sneaking up on us!"

"All done!" said Trenton, snapping off the broadcaster.

"Did you make contact?" asked the girl.

"Yes," he replied, "and now we had better get out of here before some of the pirates block us off from the other side!"

"Where shall we go?" asked Quenden.

"Somewhere where we can barricade ourselves and hold them off until help arrives!"

Swiftly the four of them ran through the succession of rooms which constituted Carconte's private apartments. Trenton assisting the girl.

"Wait a minute!" shouted Sorelle as they passed a doorway.

The adventurer pressed a knob upon the wall, and down across the doorway there spread a thin veil of the violet shafts of life destroying light.

"That will hold them for a while," he said. "It will give us a start!"

Once more they continued on their way, running into three of the lunar buccaneers as they made a sharp turn in the corridor.

"Halt!" yelled one of the moon pirates, surprised at the sudden appearance of the four fugitives.

"Brentley!" exclaimed Trenton, recognizing the co-pilot of the *Interplanetary Limited* who had turned pirate rather than forfeit his life or undergo a brain operation.

"Canute and Holmes!" cried Quenden, also recognizing his fellow crew members who had gone over to the ranks of the pirates rather than risk the chance of being consigned to the atom gun or a worse fate.

"We must return you to Carconte!" said Brentley, coming out of his sudden surprise. "We are moon pirates now you know…"

"In body but not in spirit!" laughed Trenton nervously as his atom gun covered the co-pilot. "I have radioed the Earth for help; they are sending a fleet of fighting craft; are you with us, or must we fight it out here?"

Brentley and his two companions considered for a moment, possibly ruminating as to the outcome of the affair, wishing to be upon the winning side.

"How do you know they are coming?" asked Brentley suspiciously.

"Because I just radioed them!" replied the young astronaut.

"I'm willing to join forces with you…" decided Brentley. "What do you say, Holmes?"

"We'd better," replied Holmes. "And you Canute?"

"I'm with the majority," announced Canute. "We'd better dig for safety at once; they're coming!"

A howl of rage greeted their ears as the pirates were halted at the doorway of the chamber where the violet rays of light blocked their further progress, making it necessary for them to retrace their steps a considerable distance through the labyrinth of rooms and corridors in a detour of the fatal shafts of deep violet light.

"Come," said Brentley. "I know where we can maintain our best stand…"

The little band of fugitives, whose ranks had been increased to seven, now raced at top speed through the subterranean chambers of the moon, finally reaching a room that boasted heavy, massive doors of metal.

"In here!" announced Brentley, leading the way. "There are loopholes in the door from which to fire!"

"Good!" said Sorelle, as the seven fugitives took refuge within the chamber, barring shut the heavy doors.

They awaited the coming of the moon pirates, atomic pistols directed through the loopholes in readiness for the attack that was to come.

"Where's my father?" asked the girl of Jan Trenton.

The spaceship pilot with a troubled look upon his face sought vainly in his mind for some way to explain the manner in which Clarkford had met his end without shocking the girl with the horrible truth.

"Is he dead?" she asked.

"Yes," replied Trenton, his voice sinking to a whisper. "It was better so, rather than to have lived to endure the fate Hulan had in store for him. When we arrived, he was beyond rescue, and at his own request we did that which was most merciful."

The girl broke down and sobbed despairingly, her heart torn with grief, while the young astronaut did the best he could to comfort her. Finally she gained control of herself so that she could speak coherently.

"He was all I had left," she said. "My mother died seven years ago."

"Here they come!" cried Sorelle. "Let them have it!"

The moon pirates were repulsed, suffering the loss of only one man, and then followed a gun duel of pot shots taken at one another, neither side scoring any hits, due to the fact that both factions were overcautious. This satisfied the group of fugitives, for they were only stalling for time.

"We're sunk!" exclaimed Holmes suddenly. "Look what they've got!"

"The ray gun!" exclaimed Quenden.

"They're turning it on the door!" cried Sorelle.

"Quick, out this other door!" said Brentley. "We can't stay here any longer!"

And it was true. Already, several large holes appeared in the heavy metal door as the destructive ray penetrated their stronghold. Firing a few parting shots, they prepared to leave by way of the other door. As Brentley swung it open, the fugitives gave a gasp of dismay at the sight they beheld. Standing silently outside, awaiting just such a move upon the part of the fugitives, stood the pale countenanced Nez Hulan, the human robot, a grim, cruel smile distorting his death-like features below the aluminum cranium and forehead. With him were three more of the moon pirates. He leveled a steel arm at Brentley in a denunciatory manner.

"So we have another traitor—and so soon!" he rasped.

From the metal palm of his hand there shot a yellow ray of light which burned a clean-cut hole clear through the chest of Brentley, who fell choking, gasping and bleeding in a lifeless heap upon the floor. It had all occurred so quickly, Brentley being the first to emerge from the room. The fugitives had hardly gotten over their sudden surprise before the co-pilot lay dead at their feet from the terrible destroying ray that had shot from out of the mechanical arm of the ruthless machine man.

"That is what happens to all traitors or enemies of the moon pirates!" sneered Hulan.

"And to human devils!" cried Quenden, his atom pistol flashing forth several times in quick succession at the arch-villain of the moon pirates.

A dull, blank look overspread the crafty features of Hulan as with mechanical arms he gripped his vitals where the shots from the atomic pistol had taken effect, and swaying weakly he tottered and fell, dead for the second time in his career, this time irreparably so.

"That's for Clarkford!" shouted Quenden exultantly, as several shots from the moon pirates entered his own body.

Quenden swayed slightly as death crept over him, but as he fell, his spitting pistol claimed the lives of two more of the space buccaneers, and he died bravely fighting to the last. His inanimate form slumped across the dead form of the man he had sworn to kill, the mechanical-limbed demon who had been recalled to life without a soul.

A single moon pirate blocked their progress, and a shot from Sorelle's gun disposed of the remaining buccaneer.

"Get out of here quick before more of them come!" cried Sorelle.

The five remaining fugitives fled from the room, which the moon pirates were about to enter, having cut the metal door to pieces with the ray gun. Down the corridor they sped, entering yet another room.

"The elevator!" exclaimed Canute excitedly. "The surface suits are above! We can escape to the surface of the moon! There are two elevators: one with an air lock at the foot of the shaft, while this one has an air lock at the top."

"Pile into the car!" exclaimed Trenton. "I'll hold off the pirates until you get it started!"

The buccaneers in the meantime had entered the chamber just quitted by their recent captives and had discovered the bodies of Hulan and his men, as well as those of Brentley and Quenden. On they came, down the corridor toward the room in which the five were attempting to escape to the surface. The loud voice of Carconte urged on his men with vile threats and foul language, bemoaning the loss of Hulan's brain power.

The blue streak from Jan Trenton's pistol halted the rush of the moon pirates who discreetly halted, not one of them wishing to sacrifice himself that the rest might accomplish the subjection of their late prisoners. In the elevator car the rest of the fugitives attempted to solve the problem of the elevator's locomotion, its operation being based on radical principles evolved by Hulan. The astronaut held off the moon pirates. Finally, Sorelle found the means by which the car was made to ascend, and with a jerk the car started upward only to be checked by the adventurer who called to the astronaut to get in.

CHAPTER TEN
The Earth Ships

JAN TRENTON leaped into the elevator car, which began to climb upward, while behind him the villainous band of space buccaneers under the command of the dark visaged Carconte, whose bald head bore a deep bruise, rushed down upon the elevator lobby just in time to see the bottom of the car disappearing out of sight above them.

Rapidly the car ascended, bearing the four men and girl toward the surface.

"Where does this thing stop?" asked Sorelle.

"There are some upper chambers with an air lock and surface suits up here some place," said Holmes.

The elevator car continued onward, gaining speed and acceleration of its own mechanism. Finally it slowed to a stop and the fleeing fugitives stepped out into a room in which the moon surface suits hung in a neat row upon their hangers.

"I've worn this sort of thing before," said Sorelle.

"So have I," remarked the astronaut, "but not under such pressing circumstances as these."

The five hastily donned the surface suits, Trenton assisting the girl into one of the clumsy accoutrements with its huge helmet. They then entered the air-lock chamber, after which they made their way along the narrow tunnel leading upward on a gradual ascent, bringing them to the platform deep within the moon crater.

Looking upward, they could perceive the mysterious grandeur of the dazzling sunlight where it struck the ragged lip of the crater, throwing into relief a chaos of illuminated spots and sharp-etched shadows.

"Climb upward!" directed the astronaut, pointing to the ladder that ran up the side of the crater. "The girl will follow you; I'll come last..."

Up through the blackness towards the sunlit crags of the moon crater's rugged lip, the five fugitives climbed to escape the wrath of the avenging buccaneers.

"I'm dizzy," complained the girl through the radiophone in her helmet to the astronaut below her. "My head feels light, and I must cling tight or I'll fall!"

"It's the sudden change from the gravity of the Earth to that of the moon," replied Trenton. "While we were in the moon chambers of the pirates we were under the same attraction of gravity as on the Earth, the floors of the rooms being composed of the same gravitational substance we use in the space flyer. The sensation will soon wear off when your body becomes a little more accustomed to the sudden reduction of gravity. You have never been on the surface of the moon before, have you?"

"No," replied the girl.

"You should visit Phobos and Deimos some time," said the young astronaut, trying to divert the girl's mind from the seriousness of their present situation by referring to the two tiny satellites of Mars. "If you give too hard a jump upon Deimos you'll never come back, but will continue right off into space."

Ever upward they continued their ascent, finally emerging into the brilliant sunlight upon the crater lip that overlooked the dreary, funereal aspect of the moon's surface. It was a weird, beautiful panorama of melancholy loneliness, which stretched away to the horizon whose sharp cut features stood out clearly where it met the blackness of space, studded with its fiery, scintillating galaxy of far-off suns and worlds. At another time the five fugitives would have stood spellbound at the sight, momentarily entranced by the scene spread out before them, but they were gambling with death, their lives being at stake.

"Between here and the Earth help is supposed to be on the way!" said Sorelle. "I only hope they arrive in time!"

"It's curtains for us if they don't," Holmes muttered. "Let's dig for shelter; the pirates will be after us if we stay here…"

In wide jumps and awkward hops, the five began their descent of the rise, which led to the crater's edge. The girl, unaccustomed to moon travel by foot, landed in an ungainly heap upon her side after having leaped some twenty feet or more into the air in an effort to clear an obstructing protrusion of rock about five feet high. A startled shriek rang in the ears of the four men as the girl started rolling and bouncing towards the edge of a deep crevice that yawned below them! With a headlong leap, Jan Trenton seized the girl upon the very brink of the unterminable abyss. Unable to check his impetus in order to halt his and the girl's fall into the lunar crevice, he gave an added push with his feet in a superhuman effort to bridge the awful gap with his human burden! The other side of the gulf represented a jump of some thirty feet, which the astronaut ordinarily would have consummated with ease, but with the added weight of the girl it was a different matter. Across the unknown depths of the gulf the bodies of the two shot, while their three companions held their breath in horror. Would they make it?

Upon the verge of the ragged pit, Jan Trenton, unable to check his headlong flight, had put every ounce of strength into that push, which now carried the two out over the moon crevice. His free arm stretched outward as he saw that they were going to fall short of the other side. The claws at the extremity of the arms in the surface suit were ready to grasp frantically at the smallest protuberance that might save them from the jaws of death, which awaited in the semblance of the jagged rocks of the gloomy pit's bottom far below. They struck the opposite wall of the wide crevice several feet below the top ridge. Jan Trenton clinging desperately to the rough surface with one arm and hand. With the other arm he grasped the girl firmly. Once more the ancient proverb of "fortune favors the brave" had justified itself, for the astronaut had grasped at a rough outcropping that firmly checked their further descent. It took but slight inertia for them to leap up over the edge of the pit's mouth.

"You have done so much for me already, and now I owe you my life," said the girl. "How can I ever repay you?"

"By taking my hand, and allowing me to assist you over the more dangerous stretches of the moon's surface," said Trenton.

The other three now leaped over the deep abyss, which had nearly claimed the lives of their two companions, and were at their sides.

"We must find a place of refuge in which to hide until the spaceships from Earth arrive," said Sorelle.

"They should be here by now," replied the astronaut. "Perhaps they're looking for us. I was unable to give them a very accurate estimate of our location. I noticed that the spot where we descended into the crater is not a very great distance from the Grisenwald Mountains, and that was the only clue to our location I could give them."

"There's the place to hide until they come!" exclaimed Canute. "See! That peak—it appears to be hollow!"

"Good enough!" said Trenton, starting for the designated peak in company with the girl to whose arm he clung, guarding her from the dangers that threatened the uninitiated who attempted moon travel for the first time.

Rapidly, the five ascended the steep grade in long hops and leaps that would have appeared prodigious upon the Earth, the spiked shoes of their surface suits gripping the crags of the slope securely.

"There they come!" wailed Holmes just before the five fugitives succeeded in gaining the sanctuary of the peak.

Looking behind them, Jan Trenton saw two men in surface suits standing upon the lip of the moon crater that led to the rendezvous of the lunar buccaneers, while several more were joining them from the interior. Excitedly they pointed to their recent prisoners, who were just disappearing within the shallow cavity of the peak they had climbed.

Several of them raised their atom pistols and fired—at a distance of some five hundred feet or more. Without a sound, Canute stiffened and pitched backward, his lifeless body rolling into a rough formation of calcareous outgrowth where it lodged firmly between two rocky protuberances.

Trenton, Sorelle, and Holmes hurried into the protecting hollow of the eminence, the astronaut conducting the girl to safety.

The three men then removed their atom pistols from the pockets of the surface suits where they had placed them before attempting the arduous ascent of the long ladder out of the crater. Awkwardly, they attempted the manipulation of the guns with the ungainly, steel claws that terminated the arms of the surface suits.

"How do you work these guns with the claws?" queried Holmes.

"I guess you don't," replied Sorelle. "But the pirates seem to operate them without trouble. They shot one of us!"

"I've got it!" exclaimed Trenton, who had been examining the extremities of the arms in his surface suit. "You don't need to hold atom guns in these claws—there are atom guns in the right arm of each suit! They're built-in affairs!"

"Well, I'll be—" exploded Sorelle as he stared amazedly at the small muzzle, which protruded a short distance from the arm of his surface suit, being located between the steel claws. "How do you fire them?"

With that little button inside your sleeve, just above the claw controls," replied Trenton.

Sorelle needed no more instructions, but was soon firing away at the pirates who stood boldly in plain sight upon the crater's rim. One of them toppled backward into the depths of the lunar pit before the rest discreetly hid themselves behind rough outcroppings of jagged rock. Then ensued a duel in which no more lives were claimed, consisting of a game of fire and duck, the blue flashes from behind the rocks of the dead satellite marking the positions of the moon pirates.

"They're sneaking up on us!" said Holmes.

"That's all right," replied the young astronaut. "They can get to the foot of this rise and no farther. We can hold them off for a long time. If they try to rush us, we'll mow them down."

Anxiously the young astronaut scanned the star-lit sky in which the sun shone like a flaming sphere, its corona leaping outward from the incandescent mass for several hundred thousand miles. Where were the rescue ships from the planet that rolled on its way nearly a quarter million miles away from the other side of the moon? Why didn't they come?

They were nowhere in sight.

"The pirates are coming closer?" asked Suzette Clarkford.

"They can come no farther," said Jan Trenton. "There are no more barriers behind which they can hide. To come any nearer they must show themselves."

"We're doomed!" yelled Holmes. "There isn't a chance for us now!"

The man pointed to a great, black object that was rising slowly out of the moon crater.

"The pirate spaceship!" swore Bret Sorelle. "We're trapped like rats…"

The black hulk of the *Jolly Roger,* its white skull and cross bones glaring menacingly at the four survivors of the *Interplanetary Limited,* crept up out of the crater. Slowly it rose above the ragged edges of the crater's rim, until it rode high over the jagged formations that lined the circle of the lunar cone. Its ghastly yellow disintegrator ray now shone dismally from beneath the hull of the pirate spaceship as it headed for the doomed men and girl.

With a yell of fright, Holmes leaped over the edge of the cup-like depression of the rocky peak that held the four remaining fugitives. While he was still in the air on his first leap a dozen shots from the atom guns of the pirates hidden upon the moon surface found their mark on his body, and when he landed, his inanimate form rolled limply down the side of the hill and out of sight into a narrow cleft at the foot.

Tensely, the two men and the girl awaited the ray that would send them into oblivion as the spaceship hovered near them. It was evident that from the attempts to shoot them down, the pirates were bent on destroying them, and even had they been given the opportunity to have surrendered, they would have fought to the death, preferring such a welcome end rather than that which lay in store for them at the hands of the moon pirates.

Suzette snuggled comfortably within the protecting arms of Jan Trenton.

"Goodbye," she said. "You have been so brave and good. Would it be a comfort to you before you die to know that I love you?"

"You love me?" cried the young astronaut, looking through the transparent front of their helmets down into her sweet face, joyfully oblivious to the approaching doom that hovered ever nearer, granting them a love of but a moment before the destructive ray would sweep them into the arms of death.

"Yes..." replied the girl. "Even when I first met you. And my regard for you has grown ever since."

"I've known you scarcely any time, yet it seems ages," answered the young astronaut. "I didn't dare to love you when I first saw you, even though my heart cried out for you, because I thought you were beyond my reach."

"Love is greater than all else," said the girl, nestling closer to the spaceship pilot. "It can overcome everything—even death..."

"I wonder," mused the astronaut as he gazed above to where the ugly spaceship hovered above them, its ray sweeping gradually up the side of the rise.

"Well, we three held them off together until the end," exclaimed Sorelle in farewell. "See you later..."

As the deathly shaft of yellow destruction came stealing to the edge of their stronghold, Jan Trenton hid the face of the girl by turning the front of her helmet against the chest of his surface suit while he lowered his head upon her helmet. Would the love this life had so cruelly denied him be his beyond the pales of death? Would she be there with him, or must he fight his way through more adventures to her side upon another plane of existence? She would be his—of that he was certain—no matter where they were.

A hoarse yell from Sorelle greeted his ears, interrupting the closing reveries of his life. Doubtless the ray had struck the brave adventurer and this was his dying cry. But someone shook him vigorously. He looked up.

"We're saved!" howled Sorelle, jumping with glee so high above the hollow interior of the peak that it would seem he was never coming down. "Look at the dirty beggars run, will you! And look over there..."

Sorelle pointed excitedly at the figures of the besieging moon pirates, who were running confusedly in all directions from their points of vantage, and then his arm swept over to a sight that the astounded eyes of Jan Trenton could hardly believe: There lay the wreck of the Jolly Roger, its sides smashed in upon the surface of the moon while above it rode several spaceships, more of them appearing rapidly out of the cosmic void!

"The Earth ships!" cried the young astronaut. "They have come—just in the nick of time!"

The bewildered eyes of the girl took in the startling scene.

"It seems unreal," she said, "as if I were dreaming this! Can it be possible?"

"I'll pinch you if you wish!" announced Sorelle joyfully.

"We have one another now, Suzette," said Trenton. "Do you still mean what you said before we were going to die?"

"Why of course!" answered the girl, her pretty eyes sparkling with love from behind the transparent facing of her helmet.

"Then you are mine..." he said.

The spaceships from Earth had blown up the pirate craft just as it was about to perpetrate its dastardly act and destroy the three remaining fugitives with its disintegrator ray. They had cruised about the vicinity of Grisenwald Mountain far above the moon, their telescopes searching for some sign of the moon pirates rendezvous; and then they had spied the buccaneers swarming out of the crater, followed by the pirate ship. A long range shot had destroyed the black craft with its hateful emblem. With the pirate ship hovering above them as it exploded, and the appearance of the fleet of armed interplanetary ships from Earth, the besieging moon pirates ran for cover within their underground stronghold.

Hulan had been killed by the incomparable marksmanship of Quenden; and Quenden had immediately afterward succumbed to the shots of the other moon pirates. Zind had also met his death at the hands of the avenging sniper, while Carconte, the pirate chieftain, had been present, with a large number of his crew, in the *Jolly Roger* when it had met its destruction at the hands of the fighting craft from the Earth. The rest of the moon pirates, disorganized, without leaders, and in the face of such a hopeless situation, did not even attempt to escape but surrendered meekly to the rescue forces, who took them into custody; their fates to be later decided by the Interplanetary Council, which resided upon the 'world between,' the planet Earth, whence all mankind had originally come.

The treasure that had been pilfered from the *Interplanetary Limited* by the buccaneers of space was placed in one of the spaceships from the Earth, to be transported to that planet where it would later be relayed to Mars. The heterogeneous collection of space flyers and the furnishings of the moon chambers were at a later date to be confiscated among the three worlds, and the terrible creations of Nez Hulan's turned over to the scientific bureaus of the three planets.

On one of the spaceships returning to the Earth, the three survivors of the grim tragedy sat in relaxation from the series of strenuous events and nerve wracking escapades they had undergone.

"Forget it!" laughed Sorelle. "You two have each other. I saw it coming on the first time you met, up in the observatory of the *Limited*. Besides, I'll be back in a few months. No need to ask what you folks will do."

The adventurer and explorer grinned understandingly, and then, noticing that he was the only one in the room besides the astronaut and the girl, made the discreet remark: "Well, I guess I'll go up in the pilot's cabin and see how we're getting along."

THE END

If you've enjoyed this book, you will not want to miss these terrific titles…

ARMCHAIR SCI-FI & HORROR DOUBLE NOVELS, $12.95 each

D-141   **ALL HEROES ARE HATED** by Milton Lesser
          AND THE STARS REMAIN by Bryan Berry

D-142   **LAST CALL FOR DOOMSDAY** by Edmond Hamilton
          HUNTRESS OF AKKAN by Robert Moore Williams

D-143   **THE MOON PIRATES** by Neil R. Jones
          CALLISTO AT WAR by Harl Vincent

D-144   **THUNDER IN THE DAWN** by Henry Kuttner
          THE UNCANNY EXPERIMENTS OF DR. VARSAG by David V. Reed

D-145   **A PATTERN FOR MONSTERS** by Randall Garrett
          STAR SURGEON by Alan E Nourse

D-146   **THE ATOM CURTAIN** by Nick Boddie Williams
          WARLOCK OF SHARRADOR by Gardner F. Fox

D-148   **SECRET OF THE LOST PLANET** by David Wright O'Brien
          TELEVISION HILL by George McLociard

D-147   **INTO THE GREEN PRISM** by A Hyatt Verrill
          WANDERERS OF THE WOLF-MOON by Nelson S. Bond

D-149   **MINIONS OF THE TIGER** by Chester S. Geier
          FOUNDING FATHER by J. F. Bone

D-150   **THE INVISIBLE MAN** by H. G. Wells
          THE ISLAND OF DR. MOREAU by H. G. Wells

ARMCHAIR SCIENCE FICTION & HORROR CLASSICS, $12.95 each

C-61   **THE SHAVER MYSTERY, Book Six**
          by Richard. S. Shaver

C-62   **CADUCEUS WILD**
          by Ward Moore & Robert Bradford

ARMCHAIR MYSTERY-CRIME DOUBLE NOVELS, $12.95 each

B-1   **THE DEADLY PICK-UP** by Milton Ozaki
         KILLER TAKE ALL by James O. Causey

B-2   **THE VIOLENT ONES** by E. Howard Hunt
         HIGH HEEL HOMICIDE by Frederick C. Davis

B-3   **FURY ON SUNDAY** by Richard Matheson
         THE AGONY COLUMN by Earl Derr Biggers

THE ALIENS LURKED...ON THE DARK SIDE OF THE MOON!

Back in the 1930s when Harl Vincent's wonderful Callisto saga was published, gigantic telescopes of enormous power had been in use for many years. They had helped mankind study all the heavenly orbs within our Solar System in great detail. Even in those days, fairly good charts of the Lunar and Martian surfaces had been carefully plotted. But at that time, Earth's scientists were essentially clueless about what lay on the other side of the moon, and they concluded—rightfully so—that only a trip into space could ever help us solve the mysteries of the moon's hidden side

In this non-stop, classic space opera yarn, Harl Vincent gave us that trip to the moon, along with some of the most rousing space battles ever put on paper. The Armchair Fiction edition of "Callisto at War" (originally published as two separate yet wholly connected novelettes) is a gallivanting roller coaster ride into the wilds of outer space.

ABOUT HARL VINCENT:

Harl Vincent was born Harl Vincent Schoepflin in Buffalo, New York on October 19th, 1893. In addition to being a fine writer of science fiction pulp tales, he was also a mechanical engineer for the Westinghouse Corporation and was responsible for the installation and testing of various large electrical devices.

Vincent was married to Ruth Hoff, and the couple eventually became a family of four, giving birth to both a son and daughter.

Harl Vincent's writing career began not long after he became a fan of Hugo Gernsback's legendary science fiction magazine, *Amazing Stories.* Vincent eventually became a regular fiction contributor to the magazine, a relationship that would last through the 1930s and into the early 1940s. "The Golden Girl of Munan," which first appeared in the June 1928 issue of *Amazing,* was Vincent's first published story. Over a span of fourteen years, Vincent published more than seventy science fiction stories in magazines like *Amazing* and *Astounding Stories.* "Power," "Red Twilight," "Barton's Island," and "Faster than Light" were some of his best known tales.

Although he turned away from writing in the early 1940s, Vincent always remained active in the field of science fiction, attending conventions and joining various genre-oriented clubs or societies.

After having published no science fiction or fantasy stories in well over twenty years, Vincent returned to the writing scene in 1966 with the publication of his novel, *"The Doomsday Planet."* It was only two years later that Harl Vincent died, on May 5th, 1968.

CALLISTO AT WAR

By
HARL VINCENT

Illustrated by
Leo Morey

ARMCHAIR FICTION
PO Box 4369, Medford, Oregon 97504

*For more information about Armchair Books and products, visit our
website at…*

www.armchairfiction.com

Or email us at…

armchairfiction@yahoo.com

PART ONE

"Explorers of Callisto"

CHAPTER ONE
Signals from the Moon

"THERE is no need of searching for further evidence, Ray. This is conclusive proof of your suspicion."

"It certainly looks that way, Gary. But who will believe that beings exist on the moon who could transmit such messages?"

Ray Parsons, experimenter and inventor, gazed quizzically at his friend Gary Walton, chief engineer of the great International Communications Corporation.

"Oh, they won't believe us," laughed Walton. "But neither did we believe that Mars and Venus were inhabited until a few short years ago."

"This is different. It was long conceded by astronomers that both of those planets had atmospheres and that conditions were generally such that there was the possibility of some sort of life existing on their surfaces. But the moon shows no evidence of this possibility when viewed through our super-telescopes. It has no atmosphere at all, or at least any atmosphere is so rare as to be negligible. The extremes of heat and cold further preclude the possibility of it being inhabited."

"Be that as it may, we have here some facts that cannot be overlooked or contradicted."

Gary Walton tapped the several rolls of paper tape that reposed on his desktop. They had retired to Walton's office for a talk after almost thirty-six hours of continuous work in the research laboratory of the corporation whose engineering department was presided over by Gary. The rolls of tape contained messages in an unfamiliar dot and dash code.

"Yes, I know," replied the inventor. "Those messages were undoubtedly transmitted by intelligent beings, though we have no means of decoding them. It is comparatively easy to show that the code is a real means of communication, that there are thirty-seven separate characters recurring with varying frequency, and that nineteen of these characters are the same as certain of those used in Continental Morse. This should prove the existence of a language and a code foreign to our Earth—the spaces between letters—the longer spaces between words, and all that. The world might easily believe that the messages come from another planet, but not from the moon—the body whose surface has been most closely examined and on which we are certain there is no life."

"But the readings of the direction finders?"

Ray's brow creased in perplexity. "That is the strange part of it," he said. "Our indications are definite. We have followed the signals for many hours and the shifting of our loops has kept constantly in line with our satellite. The signals cannot have come from any other point, excepting by reflection."

"Reflection! Fiddlesticks!" snorted Walton. "You know as well as I do that such signals, if they could reach us from another planet by reflection from the moon, would also reach us directly and a line could be obtained on their original source with our direction finders. No, Ray, you are arguing against your own convictions. These signals come from the moon."

"But how? Doggone it, Gary, when Lesser invented the super-telescope in 1952, the first thing he examined was the surface of the moon. With the tremendous magnifying power it would be possible to see a sparrow on the moon's surface, but he saw nothing living. And nothing living has been observed in the fifteen years during which his instrument has been in use all over the world. Life has been found on Mars and on Venus. There is a fair evidence of its existence on certain of the satellites of Jupiter and Saturn. But—on the moon—never."

"Nevertheless you must admit that now, messages came from that supposedly uninhabited satellite."

"Yes," admitted Parsons, slowly, "they did. But, by all that's good and holy, I can't account for it. And neither can you."

The young inventor sat slouched in his chair, disheveled and weary. He was bewildered and disgruntled over the findings of the recent experiments in which he had requested the aid of the older man. True, they had proved to their own satisfaction the points they had set out to determine. Ray had reached a similar conclusion previously in his own workshop, but had hoped that the more powerful apparatus in the laboratory of the great organization, in whose New York headquarters he now sat, would show his original data to be erroneous. It was too preposterous! He would not dare to publish his findings on account of the storm of protest that would come from the great scientists with whom he was already at loggerheads. Suddenly he pulled himself up and laughed.

"By George, Gary," he said, "this thing has me cuckoo. But, as you say, I'm convinced of the correctness of our results. And I'm going to see for myself what's on the moon before I let the word out on these experiments."

"Through the telescope?"

"No siree. I'm going to go there and look around."

It was Gary Walton's turn to stare. "Going there?" he gasped. "How?"

"Haven't the slightest idea. But I'll build myself a ship of some kind that'll get me there."

"What's the advantage? We can already observe the surface as if from a distance of less than three hundred feet by means of our telescopes. Why run the risk of losing your life in some hare-brained attempt at shooting yourself there in a rocket or something like that?"

"Don't worry about me. If I start I am going to get there—and back. And I do expect to find something."

"Where? In some fancied underground realm?"

Ray laughed once more. "Now who's the kill-joy?" he inquired. "A few minutes ago you were on the other side of the argument."

The older man grinned. "Oh, go ahead," he said, "you'll have your own way no matter how much I argue. But promise me you will take me along."

"Sure thing. And I'm not joking about it, either."

"Neither am I."

They gripped hands solemnly.

"Now, what do you say we go home and knock off a little sleep?" suggested Walton.

"Best idea you've had since day before yesterday. Let's go."

They indulged in much good-natured banter as they washed up and prepared to leave the deserted building. It was well toward morning when Gary locked the door of his office behind them and they had a considerable wait for the night elevator to rise from the street floor to the ninety-fourth, on which the office and laboratory were located.

The night watchman was accustomed to the late comings and goings of the two, so he made no remarks regarding the lateness of the hour. But when, at the thirtieth floor or thereabouts, Ray let forth a yell like a Comanche, he was so startled that he let go of the controller handle.

"What's the matter?" asked Gary, in real concern.

"I've got it! By George, I've got it!"

"Got what?"

"The solution!" he babbled, excitedly. "What dumbbells we are not to have thought of it before. The other side—the other side of the moon. That's where the transmitter is."

"The other side?" said Gary blankly.

"Sure. We only see the side that is toward the Earth and that is always the same. Who knows what is on the other side, the side that is always turned from us?"

The watchman gaped as the two capered like schoolboys and, when they left the elevator at the main floor, he scratched his head and watched as they scampered through the long hall to the exit of the building.

"Bug-house, the two of them," he said in deep conviction.

CHAPTER TWO
The Meteor

DURING the succeeding four months Gary Walton saw almost nothing of his friend and whenever he reached him by radiophone he was refused permission to visit the laboratory where Ray was so busily engaged.

"No, Gary old man," was the burden of his refrain. "I have some ideas of my own I am following in the construction of this ship, and I'm just not going to let anyone in on it until I'm sure it's going to come up to expectations."

"But, can't I help?" Gary would ask.

"Not a bit. Everything is going fine and there is nothing I need. So please quit worrying about it."

"But I'm getting anxious."

"I know you are," Ray would laugh, "but you won't have long to wait, and I can promise you something quite different from what you might expect."

Further argument proved useless in each case and Gary finally gave it up as a bad job. But he grew more impatient as time passed and when Ray ultimately notified him that all was in readiness he hastened to Grand Central Terminal and boarded the first train that would take him to the small hamlet in Monroe County where Ray's laboratory was located.

Ray Parsons was an unusual figure in the scientific world. At his graduation from college he had spent two years wandering about the world with nothing to do but play. Instead of playing, however, he seized the opportunity of visiting the great universities and research laboratories of Europe, there conferring with scientists of note and occasionally making a stop of several weeks to assist in some particularly interesting work that happened to be under way. The young man's wealth and ability found him a welcome abroad and he learned much during this period, incidentally contributing not a little of his own knowledge and downright genius.

He was recalled to New York at the untimely death of his father and found himself an orphan, possessed of more riches than he knew what to do with. The money he promptly forgot, excepting as a means to an end, and he straightaway set about indulging himself in his hobby—science. He equipped one of the finest private laboratories in the United States and, with a few assistants, buried himself in the work he had chosen. The succeeding ten years saw his rise to the position of an authority of note—an authority of such preeminence that he was continually subject to the critical and oft times caustic animadversions of the savants who envied him his notable accomplishments. But he remained unspoiled by praise and unperturbed by criticism.

Gary Walton mused on these things as his train sped northward. His own case was quite different. Reared in poverty, he had been forced to start working at an early age and had worked hard ever since. He was forty-six, just ten years older than Ray, and had already rolled up thirty years of experience that had begun with the clerkship in the office of the first organization to commercialize television-radio and bring it into the homes of the nation. From this small beginning he had struggled upward, growing up with the organization as it eventually merged with and obtained control of the wire and cable companies, the various broadcasting and commercial radio corporations, until it finally emerged as the sole owner and operator of all communication systems in use on Earth. His experience, though in a specialized line, was highly valuable and the reward for his years of hard work and self-education came in the not to be despised position he now held.

When his train slowed down at the station he caught a glimpse of Ray's low-slung red roadster and the smile on the face of the inventor apprised him of the fact that another engineering triumph had been achieved.

"Welcome to our city," Ray greeted him, when he had swung across the platform and approached the car.

"Thanks," grunted Gary, feigning sarcasm. "I'm welcome now that the work is done, eh?"

"Not sore, are you?"

Ray's eyes twinkled. He knew that his friend hated being left out of anything until the last moment.

"Of course not—really. But you might at least have told me what you were doing."

He climbed in beside his grinning friend and they were soon rolling along the main thoroughfare of the town and headed for the outskirts.

The laboratory was a rambling group of buildings, some frame, some brick, and a few of molded concrete. These were set well back from the road about a mile from town and were separated from the neighboring farmhouses by broad rolling fields that comprised the property Ray had purchased after his father's demise. Gary noted that a considerable area to the rear of the buildings had been walled off by a high board-fence whose eight-foot top was surmounted by several lines of glistening barbed wire.

"Got the ship well hidden, haven't you?" he commented as the car pulled up on the gravel drive alongside the new fence.

"You bet! And we're going to keep it hidden until we have all the dope on these strange messages. By the way, have there been any more?"

"Yes. Every five days, as regular as clockwork, they begin at midnight and transmit for one hour and twenty minutes. They seem to have a regular schedule now and I have a whole roomful of tape. Don't know what we are ever going to do with it all, unless we toss it out of the window when there is another hero-parade up Broadway."

"Well, we're going to learn who is working the transmitter up there on the moon, anyway."

Ray inserted his key in the lock of a heavy door in the fence as he spoke. When he swung this door open Gary gasped at what he saw at the near end of the enclosed field.

"Why, it's nothing but an airplane!" he exclaimed.

"With a few important differences," his friend conceded.

And the *Meteor,* as Ray had christened the vessel, did indeed resemble a standard high-speed enclosed plane. The body was some forty feet in length, torpedo-shaped and surmounted by a single wing-structure that seemed ridiculously small and of unusual thickness on the leading edge. Not more than twenty feet from wing tip to wing tip did this plane measure. The landing gear was not unusual, comprising the regulation rubber-tired wheels and tailskid. The tail structure was likewise of conventional design with fins and rudder that might have come from the shop of one of the standard airplane manufacturers. At the nose there showed the standard propeller of gleaming bakelite. The body was of polished metal with the exception of numerous circular windows that seemed to be of extremely thick glass. Surrounding the tapered tail and blunt nose of the body there were a number of cylinders of about six inches diameter and eight feet in length. These looked for all the world like the barrels of small cannon and gave the craft a warlike appearance. There was not a strut or a guy wire to mar the symmetry of the whole or to destroy the impression of indestructible rigidity presented by the sleek craft.

"Isn't she a beauty?" asked Ray enthusiastically.

"Sure is. But what makes it go?"

CHAPTER THREE
Thoroughly Equipped

THE short, rotund figure of an overalled man emerged from a circular hatch and dropped to the ground.

"Eddie Dowling," said Ray. "He's going with us."

"Fine business. Anyone else?"

"No, just we three." He turned and addressed the mechanic. "Come here, Eddie."

"Oh, hello Walton. I hear you're going with us."

This from the smiling-faced, chubby Dowling, who wiped his hands on a piece of cotton waste as he advanced.

"Hello, Eddie. Haven't seen you in a year. Yes, I'm going along—think we'll get there?" said Gary.

The smiling countenance became owlishly solemn. "Positively. Wait till you see this ship. She's a corker."

Dowling went to the shop for some tools and Ray and Gary climbed through the circular hatch into a small chamber inside the vessel. This chamber formed an air lock and communicated with the interior through a second circular hatch.

The center compartment of the *Meteor* was about fifteen feet in diameter and of approximately the same length between the partitions separating it from the other two sections. There was a periscope arrangement that provided an unobstructed view ahead and to the rear from the pilot's seat. The circular windows in the double cellular hull gave vision in all other directions. There were four bunks, two upper and two lower, besides two comfortably upholstered double seats and a small table that folded in beside the bunks. The rest of this chamber was cluttered with the controls and a mass of complicated mechanisms, most of which were entirely unfamiliar to Gary.

In the forward compartment there was the fifteen-cylinder radial engine and its fuel supply, the motor being of six hundred horsepower rating. The rear compartment contained the heating, refrigerating and air conditioning apparatus as well as the supply of provisions and other stores required in the trip. Altogether it was an over-crowded interior, though neat and orderly withal.

Ray pressed a button as Gary sank into the cushions of one of the divan-like seats. There was the whine of a motor coming up to speed and the engineer gazed inquiringly at his friend as a strange feeling crept over him.

"Stand up," Ray commanded with a twinkle in his eye.

And he laughed boyishly as Gary struggled against an unseen force in the effort to rise to his feet. It seemed that his weight had grown enormous and he was barely able to pull himself to an erect position.

"What in the world is this?" he asked in astonishment.

"Artificial gravity. You see, when we leave the immediate neighborhood of good old mother Earth, her attraction will become less and less until eventually we would be floating about, unable to control our movements, were it not for this feature of the *Meteor*. By its means we can maintain normal gravity when out in space. Here on Earth your weight is just about doubled now, I also have a similar apparatus for overcoming the effects of acceleration and deceleration, which might otherwise prove fatal to our bodily structure."

He cut off the energy and Gary sank to his feet with a sigh of relief.

"Why, that's wonderful, Ray," he said. "Something new?"

"No, I have been working on it for years and this is as far as I have gotten in the effort to discover means of nullifying our gravity. I can't seem to reverse the process."

"You are using your own fuel in the motor?"

"Yes indeed. The new concentrate that shows ninety thousand B. T. U. per pound. We have almost enough aboard to carry us around the world."

"But that will only carry us one-tenth of the way to the moon."

"Less than that, if we used it. But the motor will be used only while we are in the Earth's atmosphere, so we have far more of the concentrate than we need. The propeller and wings are useless, you know, out in the near vacuum of space. There is nothing for them to work on. When we leave the atmosphere we shall depend on the rocket tubes—those cylinders surrounding the nose and tail."

"How do they operate?"

"By the reactive effect of successively fired charges of Parsonite, my super-explosive. And these tubes may be swung about in various directions so that we can steer the vessel and progress in any direction at will. They will also be used in landing on the moon's surface. If, as is supposed, there is little or no atmosphere, the wings and propeller would avail us nothing, so we will be compelled to retard the ship by means of properly directed discharges from the rocket tubes and thus land safely."

"But suppose there are living beings on the other side of the moon and that they attack us. Have you weapons and means of defense?"

"Absolutely. Of course we have no means of knowing what sort of weapons might be used against us but with a race of beings of great enough intelligence to make use of the powerful radio signals we picked up, it will likely be some form of destructive ray. The hull of the *Meteor* and the specially cast glass of the windows are proof against such attack. Of course if they use projectiles we are out of luck, but I hardly consider that likely. We likewise have several forms of destructive rays of our own, flame pistols, and a short wave projector that produces fusing heat in metal objects at a considerable distance."

"How can the flame pistols be used? We're not going to leave the *Meteor* when on the moon's surface, are we?"

"Surely. How else could we accomplish anything?"

"But how can we leave the ship if there is no atmosphere and if the temperature at night is some two hundred degrees below zero, as is estimated by astronomers?"

"Don't you know me better than that by this time?" Ray laughed. "Those things have all been anticipated. We'll leave through the air locked entrance and return the same way. There are three suits in the rear compartment that are airtight and provided with oxygen helmets like diving suits. Woven in the materials of these suits there are innumerable fine wires that will pick up short wave energy broadcast from the *Meteor* and convert it into heat to keep us comfortable in the lunar cold. We'll have weapons in our belts and everything necessary, including miniature radios in the helmets so that we can converse up to a distance of a half mile."

"I give up," said Gary helplessly. "There is nothing you do not think of. And I can offer no further objections. When do we go?"

"Can you make it the day after tomorrow?"

"Sure thing. I'll return tonight and get things in shape at home, pack my bag, and be here at whatever time you say."

"All right then. Suppose you take the early morning train and we'll figure on taking off at noon."

"Right. And how long is the trip going to take?"

"Some ten or eleven hours. Of course we can't say how long we might remain there, but better figure on being away no less than a week."

Ray chuckled at the expression of amazement that spread over Gary's lean features.

"Ten or eleven hours," he gasped. "How fast does the *Meteor* travel?"

"I calculate on a maximum of about fifty thousand miles an hour. We can accelerate gradually to this speed after leaving our atmosphere, then decelerate gradually with a resulting average of more than half of that speed."

Gary shook his head slowly. "Seems impossible," he said. "But I'll believe you, and will be johnny-on-the-spot when the time comes."

CHAPTER FOUR
The Meteor in Space

At the appointed time the three adventurers ensconced themselves in the center compartment of the *Meteor*, the outer hatch being bolted securely from the inside. There were no witnesses in the enclosed field and no news of their projected journey had leaked out to the press or news broadcasters. Everything was in readiness and Eddie Dowling mounted the pilot's seat with a grin that spread from ear to ear. He had piloted the ship on a trial the preceding evening and was so enthused and so anxious to get out of the upper reaches of the atmosphere that he could scarcely wait for Ray's signal to start.

In the view plate of the periscope there appeared the broad expanse of the field ahead and the high board fence at the far end, beyond which there was a clump of trees.

"Think she'll clear the woods with this load, Eddie?" asked Ray.

"Sure. Cleared it a mile last night, and there isn't five hundred pounds extra on board now."

"You should know. Let her go then."

"Right-o!"

Eddie yanked the starter lever as if he wished to pull it from its socket. There was a grinding roar up front, then the smooth purr of the motor. Faster and faster spun the propeller. Then he pulled another lever, which released the brakes below them, and they started rolling down the field. As the powerful motor picked up speed under full throttle, its exhaust gases being discharged almost noiselessly to the rear through the long pipes that hung beneath the streamlined body, they sped more and more swiftly until the tail was up. Then the wheels were clear and, with a sharp rise that carried them well over the fence and trees. They were off!

The *Meteor* climbed at a steep angle in Eddie's eagerness to gain altitude quickly and in less than five minutes the altimeter registered twenty thousand feet. Soon it showed thirty thousand feet, then forty and the speed of the motor had increased perceptibly while the ship seemed to be climbing more slowly.

"Air's getting pretty rare outside," Ray explained at Gary's questioning glance. "Pretty soon the propeller won't take hold at all and we'll have to use the rocket tubes."

It was the day of the new moon and, at the angle they climbed, its orb was visible in the periscope screen. They were heading directly for their destination. Before long the altimeter needle had reached the end of the scale and Ray placed in operation two instruments of his own design.

These were distance and speed indicators, which depended on the Earth's attraction for their operation, rather than on the barometric pressure as in the case of the standard altimeter. So condensed were the scales of these instruments at the lower readings that the needles scarcely flickered with their comparatively slow speed and nearness to the Earth. The stick and rudder-bar wobbled loosely at the touch of Eddie's hand and feet. The air resistance was approaching zero and the motor raced alarmingly.

"Cut the throttle, Eddie," ordered Ray, "and give her about a ten second burst from the rear rocket tubes."

The motor coughed and died. Eddie turned to a panel with a number of buttons arranged like the keys of a typewriter. He pressed five or six of these and there came a blast of rapid, staccato barks from the rear. Gary had a sensation of being suddenly thrown through space with tremendous velocity but this passed immediately as the acceleration compensating energy responded. He looked through one of the circular windows in the floor and exclaimed aloud at what he saw. The Earth, which had but a moment previously been a huge bowl, was now a perfect globe of enormous size that receded rapidly as he watched. He could scarce drag his eyes from the marvelous sight, but turned quickly at a shout from Ray and Eddie. The speed indicator registered eight thousand miles an hour and the needle was moving steadily to the right over the scale whose highest graduation was at one hundred thousand miles an hour!

"Glory be!" shouted Eddie. "She's even faster than you figured, Chief. Man alive—we're traveling!"

"No wonder," said Ray drily. "You had the rockets on for nearly a half minute."

Eddie turned a crestfallen face toward them. "So I did," he admitted sheepishly. "Good thing the compensators worked so well."

So rapid was the acceleration with no air friction to retard it, that within the hour, they had reached a velocity of nearly thirty thousand miles an hour. The trip would be completed much sooner than Ray had anticipated.

Gary watched spellbound as the Earth receded and the moon grew larger and nearer. He experienced a curious feeling of detachment as the great gleaming sphere that was their world took on a green luminescence that shone eerily against the blackness of the firmament whose stars presented the entirely new aspect of glowing brilliantly without the accustomed twinkle caused by motions of an intervening atmosphere. Ahead and to the left, the sun was a blinding blaze of magnificence, shooting great streamers of flame far into space in every direction. The moon, several times larger than it appeared from the Earth, now showed a bright, pencil-line crescent as the triangle formed by their ship, the sun, and the moon grew smaller and the angles slowly altered.

The face of the moon was in shadow but shone with a fair degree of brightness by light reflected from the Earth. But so brilliant was the sun-lit crescent at the left edge that the face seemed almost wholly dark by comparison. And steadily it drew closer.

Their speed had become constant at about thirty-five thousand miles an hour and Ray started experimenting with the tail rockets. He pressed a couple of the control buttons for an instant and the resulting discharges swung the needle well over the fifty thousand mark. Another touch and it reached seventy. They were traveling at more than a thousand miles a minute! And the interior of the *Meteor* was as comfortable and as normal as regards temperature, air quality, and gravity as if they were flying at ordinary speed and altitude over the surface of the Earth.

"Guess I was very conservative in my estimates," said Ray, "and I believe I know where I made an error. Parsonite, you know, when it is exploded on Earth, produces about four million times its own volume in expanding gases. But out here in the vacuum the specific volume of the gas is vastly greater and that makes a difference. In my calculations, of course, I considered the weight of the discharged gases and that does not change with the lowering in pressure. But the greater volume must have considerable effect since, at each explosion, we leave behind a far larger cloud against which to react. This larger cloud, while of the same weight, must have considerably greater instantaneous inertia."

"Exactly what I thought," grinned Eddie.

"Oh, of course, that is a foolish explanation, in violation of the simple law of Newton," said Ray. "The real reason for the higher speed is that a higher muzzle velocity is obtained in the rocket tubes due to the expanding of the gases to a lower pressure."

"At any rate," Gary interjected, "we are getting there pretty fast."

He had cast a glance at the instrument board and noticed that the distance from the Earth was now well over 170 thousand miles. And they were scarcely three hours out!

"Yes," agreed Ray, "and it will soon be time for a change in direction."

When they had reached the 200 thousand mile mark and the moon appeared as large before them as did the Earth behind, Ray took the controls. He swung a small lever over the face of a graduated quadrant and pressed a single button of the rocket-control keyboard. There were a few rapid, machine gun-like reports from the rear and the moon's image swung well to the left of the periscope screen.

"We'll pass it on the shadowed side," he stated.

Sun and moon were both visible through the circular windows now and it was not long until the moon's disc bit into the right side of the flaming orb and slowly started crossing. They were producing an eclipse all their own and it was a vastly different one from those witnessed on Earth. The apparent diameter of the moon was now so immense that it gradually swallowed up the sun and its long, flaming streamers as well. When they were in exact opposition with the two bodies, the *Meteor* was plunged into a baleful green semi-darkness, the sole illumination being by light reflected from the Earth and by that of the Earth re-reflected from the surface of the moon. The firmament became of ebon blackness, the brilliant points of light that were the stars and planets contributing but little to the light that streamed through their circular windows.

Then the first wavering tips of the sun's great prominences started to appear on the other side and the brilliant orb was soon in full view once more. Another twenty minutes and a crescent of brightness appeared at the moon's edge and this widened rapidly as the *Meteor* dashed through space with its speed still unchecked. The lunar orb was half illuminated and the distance from Earth showed 236 thousand miles before Ray manipulated the control buttons of the forward rocket tubes. They were passing the moon at a distance of about five thousand miles and it was of colossal size in their vision.

CHAPTER FIVE
In the Path of a Beam of Waves

RAY pressed fully half the keys on the small panel, putting all the rocket tubes at the nose in operation. Time and again he pressed the same group for a period of ten or fifteen seconds and at each pressure there was a responding rat-tat-tat and a momentary sensation of being thrown forward in the ship. The compensators worked beautifully, however, and they experienced not the slightest discomfort at the tremendous rate of deceleration. In a very short time they had considerably overshot their destination and the needle of the speed indicator had dropped well toward zero. Ray played the keyboard now like a piano and the heavens rotated before them as the *Meteor* swung around in the arc of a huge circle. Another few minutes and the sun was almost directly overhead with the lighted surface of the moon just beneath. They were looking at its other side.

From a position estimated by Ray as about two thousand miles above the surface it was quite apparent that the side they had never seen was mightily different from the face presented toward the Earth. There were a multitude of the familiar craters, several of these being even larger than Ptolemy and Copernicus. But the greater portion of the surface that now hid the Earth from view was occupied by huge areas resembling the Mare Serenitatis and the Mare Tranquilitatis but of prodigious extent and deeply depressed rather than presenting comparatively level surfaces, thus more deserving of being termed seas. From the close range the craters seemed quite likely to have been formed by the impact of meteorites when the moon was in a plastic state, as suggested by Gilbert. An intricate network of rays and rills interconnected the numerous craters and the seas, the rays gleaming with the blue-white color of polished cobalt and the rills revealing themselves as lengthy chasms and cracks of unspeakable depth. The visitors were on their knees, observing through the floor windows this marvel of creation never before seen by Earthly eyes.

A touch of a button had headed the *Meteor* in the same direction followed by the moon in its orbit and they now seemed to be hanging motionless above its surface. Actually they were traveling in space at the same speed and over the same course as the Earth's satellite.

"It's a wonderful sight, boys," said Gary solemnly.

"Marvelous," agreed Ray.

"You said something," came from Eddie.

Ray fussed with the small levers that swung the rocket tubes out radially from the hull. He pressed two of the control keys and there came a few sharp raps from overhead, both forward and to the rear. The moon seemed to leap upward to meet them and Ray manipulated various other buttons rapidly. By alternating between upper and lower tubes, he soon maneuvered the vessel to within ten or fifteen miles of the surface.

The panorama that spread before their eyes as the *Meteor* sped along at this altitude in response to Ray's further manipulations was bizarre in the extreme. They crossed a crater of fully 150 miles diameter and whose depth was no less than five miles. In the exact center of this crater there rose a slender spin of deep green hue that reached a height of probably six or seven miles above the crater's bottom. A lofty mountain range loomed ahead as they crossed the far rim of the crater—perpendicular peaks lifted their pointed finials to unconscionable altitudes.

Eddie busied himself with the mechanism of a camera, which was set flush with the floor, its lens mounted outside on the bottom of the hull. The shutter clicked incessantly as he replaced roll after roll of exposed film with fresh. Ray kept constant watch of his instruments and occasionally fired a light rocket charge below to maintain their altitude and direction of travel. Gary's optics were working overtime as they dropped to two thousand feet.

The manometer showed no atmospheric pressure outside the ship and the stopping of the heat generators and starting of the refrigerating motors caused Ray to glance at the thermometer that recorded outside temperature. It was near the boiling point!

"It is just about noon of the long lunar day," said Ray.

"Then there are about fourteen of our days to pass before there will be darkness at this point?" inquired Gary.

"That's right. And it's going to be good and hot out there in the sun as long as we're near the surface. Probably be quite a bit cooler in shadow, though, and when we leave the ship we'll have to keep to the shadows to keep from boiling."

"Are there no means of cooling the airtight suits?"

"None. But that doesn't worry me. If we can't live in the direct rays of the sun, neither can the other fellow. We'll find them in deep shade."

"Where are you going to find any shadows with the sun almost directly overhead?"

"In the larger rills at great depth or possibly under overhanging ledges at the shores of the great seas."

They now followed a ledge that shone beneath them like a vein of pure silver. They were to discover later that it was nearly unadulterated cobalt. This ledge led them through an almost level valley, fringed on both sides by the greenish spires whose material proved subsequently to be nephrite.

After an hour of travel in this manner they came to the immense bowl that was the largest of the seas they had observed from far above. It was an enormous depression and, as they crossed the near rim, it seemed they had come to the edge of the moon for the great barren concavity was as deep as fifty miles or more in spots within their range of vision. A steep, overhanging precipice marked its rim and they skirted this at moderate speed, examining the streaked wall carefully for signs of life.

Ray tuned in the radio to the wavelength on which they had received the messages back there in New York. He clapped the phones to his ears and listened intently. There were no signals, but a continual musical hum of perhaps a hundred cycles frequency assailed his eardrums. This rose and fell in volume like a fading signal but he had no way of determining from whence it came.

For two hours more they skirted the multi-colored precipice, slowing down occasionally to peer closely at strange formations that had, from a greater distance, resembled human dwellings. But there was still no sign of life.

Eddie had taken numerous photographs and he desisted from the work as the sameness of the view became all too apparent.

"We'll have lots of evidence when we get back, Chief," he smiled.

"Yes, and we'll need it, if we find no more than we have found so far in the way of a lunar radio transmitter. Wonder where the devil it is."

Noting that it was nearing midnight by Earth time, he replaced the headphones of the radio.

"Hum's gone now," he muttered.

Then he and the two other passengers were electrified by the shrill, penetrating note of continuous wave code signals that came in so loudly as to be heard throughout the compartment. Ray hastily removed the phones to save his eardrums.

"Boy! They must be close!" he exclaimed. "Either that or it is an extremely powerful transmitter, which of course it must be if it was used to communicate with one of the other planets."

"Look!" shouted Gary suddenly, from his position at one of the windows. "There it is! Ahead there to the left."

His companions peered in the direction indicated and, at the top of the cliff not a mile ahead, they saw large fan-shaped structures topping two tall metal towers. The strands of this odd antenna reflected the sun's unobstructed rays with the unmistakable reddish hue of copper wires or tubing.

"No wonder it nearly knocked my ears off," said Ray, turning off the current that fed the tubes of the radio.

He nosed the ship downward with a few carefully directed shots from the tubes and they dove into the shadow of the cliff. At first the darkness seemed to be intense but there was really a considerable amount of reflected light from the neighboring sun-lit surfaces of the arid sea bottom. As their eyes became used to the sudden change from the brilliance of the lunar midday to the twilight of this shaded region they made out a strange village ahead. It looked like the "tank farm" of an oil refinery back home. Fully forty large metallic cylinders reared themselves from the level bottom at the base of the cliffs and these were of unmistakably human design and construction. As they drew nearer they made out the forms of several bipeds who moved in and out between the habitations, walking erect in the same manner as humans of the Earth.

The first sign of life!

CHAPTER SIX
The Pursuing Lunarians

IT was necessary to fire an occasional light rocket charge and in each case the luminous gases of the explosion lighted the shaded area like a flash of lightning. It was thus but a short time until their presence was revealed to the lunar inhabitants. A great many of these tumbled from the doors of the circular dwellings and they milled about and gesticulated excitedly over the unexpected appearance of the strange ship.

On closer view it was seen that these beings were accoutered in garments very similar to those that reposed in the lockers of the rear compartment of the *Meteor*. The suits, also of pliable material, bulged ludicrously in the vacuum under pressure of the air from within and each figure was topped by an egg-shaped helmet of shiny metal.

It was difficult to maintain the position of the *Meteor* without traveling at considerable speed, for the craft bobbed about uncertainly under the influence of successive charges fired from the tubes. Ray decided to make a landing and he maneuvered the vessel to a point about a mile from the village and there dropped to the surface. At their contact there arose a cloud of gray powder that cut off their view for several minutes. With the subsequent raising of the cloud they saw that a group of the Lunarians were approaching them with great speed, and progressed in leaps that carried them thirty or forty feet at each jump. Evidently they hailed from another body in the solar system—a body whose gravity was nearly equivalent to that of the Earth, assuming the physical strength of these beings to be about equal to that of the Tellurians.

When the more curious of the beings had approached within a hundred feet of the *Meteor* they formed a semicircle and it was seen at once that each of the members of the party carried a slender rod of about four feet length, these rods being equipped with bulbous protuberances and presenting the appearance of weapons. Like a company of well-trained soldiers they raised the peculiar small arms and directed them at the *Meteor*.

"Hope our insulating envelope holds out," remarked Ray. "Those are quite evidently ray projectors of some sort."

At his words there came a blinding flare from each of the rods and their bodies were subjected to a stinging, prickling sensation that betokened a heavily charged atmosphere within the vessel. The light flashes that converged on the outer surface of the staunch craft seemed to have no other effect and Eddie whooped with glee when they saw that the Lunarians were mystified at the failure of their attack.

There came another burst of the blinding flashes after a moment and the *Meteor* lurched and tilted at an alarming angle as one of the rays took effect on the landing gear.

"Say!" exclaimed Ray. "This will never do! Suppose they shoot away our wings and landing gear entirely? We'll have some trouble in landing when we return to Earth. I'm going to try the short waves on them."

He advanced to a powerful high frequency transmitter and started its motor generator. The tubes glowed instant response and Ray swung a lever on the panel of the transmitter slowly from left to right, watching the enemy meanwhile.

"Just warming them up a bit," he explained to Gary. "Watch!"

That little transmitter, by conduction through the ether, was inducing high frequency currents of nearly a million alternations per second in the bodies of the Lunarians. Soon their bodily temperature would begin to rise and it would not be long until they were all laid low with raging fevers and racing pulses. Ray did not wish to kill any of them unless it was necessary in self-defense.

One of the Lunarians sank slowly to his knees, then rolled forward and lay prone. Others of them moved about in a bewildered manner as if searching for the cause of their sudden illness. Another dropped, then two more, and in less time than it takes to tell, they lay helpless in the heavy dust.

"Now," said Ray, "we'll go out and look them over. Our own suits are insulated against these vibrations."

Hastily they donned the heavy suits and globular helmets. Ray showed Gary how to adjust the oxygen apparatus and how to operate the various instruments that hung from the outside belt. One of these was the flame pistol with which Gary was already slightly familiar. They entered the air lock and bolted the inner hatch. Then Eddie unbolted the outer hatch and they plainly heard the hiss of the escaping air.

Eddie was first to drop into the thick powder that carpeted the ground and he took the first experimental step, tumbling into a ludicrous heap as he lost his balance in the eight-foot spring that resulted from his slight effort. It would require a little time for them to become accustomed to moving about in a gravity field only one-sixth as strong as their own.

They shuffled through the powdery footing until they reached the outstretched Lunarians. Gary kneeled over one of the prostrate forms and peered through the single window of his helmet. He recoiled at the look of hate that flashed through from the bloodshot eyes of the helpless being. But the fevered face that looked out at him was unmistakably human. With the exception of the slightly purpled skin that was probably caused by the artificially produced fever, this man might have been one of the millions that inhabited his home city on Earth. The phones in his helmet spoke loudly and he gazed up, startled at the voice of Ray that seemed to come from so close by. He was astonished at seeing the ballooned figure of his friend fully a hundred feet from him. Then he remembered the helmet radios.

"Gary," came the voice, "these people are just like our own in features and in stature."

"Yes. It seems incredible."

A sharp cry in Eddie's voice startled them both and they were still further astonished when they looked in the direction pointed to by his bloated, outstretched arm in its bulging enclosure.

About five hundred yards away, out of reach of the vibrations from the *Meteor* that still charged the ether, five of the Lunarians were chasing a sixth figure—one of their own kind. From the smaller stature and shorter leaps of the fugitive, they deduced that it was a woman, and when this one stumbled, falling heavily in the dust and burying the huge helmet in folded arms, they felt more than certain.

At that moment the pursuers caught sight of the round-helmeted strangers, the strange ship, and the prostrate forms of their own kind. They stopped short and two of them raised rods similar to those carried by the helpless victims at their feet. Eddie was nearest in line and the two flashes from the raised weapons converged in his direction. Instinctively he dodged and the impetus of his movement threw him fifteen feet from the line of fire. In a rage he grasped the flame pistol that depended from his belt and trained it on the Lunarians. There was a brilliant spurt of scarlet and one of the attackers was consumed in the angry flame that struck him full in the chest. Before the other could again bring his own weapon into pray, he, too, fell a victim to the angry Eddie. The oxygen in their own suits made brilliant torches of the two Lunarians as the deadly flame got in its work. The other three were unarmed and they fled precipitately in the direction of the village, leaving the erstwhile fugitive still cowering in the dust.

The three Tellurians advanced to the crumpled figure, which shrank from them as they drew near. Eddie placed his helmet close to the larger egg-shaped one and looked through the two intervening windows.

"By Christopher!" he exclaimed. "It's a girl! And a peach!"

By pantomime they convinced her they would not harm her and eventually got her to her feet and indicated their desire to take her within their vessel. After a considerable amount of gesturing and nodding and bowing on both sides she finally accompanied them willingly and they noticed that she shrank in alarm from the prostrate figures of her compatriots.

In a few minutes they were all four in the air-locked entrance of the *Meteor* and, when Eddie had bolted the outer hatch, they heard the welcome hiss of air entering the chamber from the pumps in the rear compartment. No sooner were they within when the girl tore her helmet from her head and threw it to the floor.

They fell back, amazed at the wild beauty that confronted them.

CHAPTER SEVEN
Communicating by Pictures

THE torrent of speech that assailed their ears might well have been a paean of praise, so softly and smoothly did the unfamiliar syllables of her euphonic language roll from her tongue. But the fire that glinted in the wondrous brown eyes and the gestures with which she supplemented the unintelligible dissertation told them she was berating her recent pursuers. With their helmets in hand the three men listened politely, but with expressions of such bewildered indetermination that the girl broke off and stared from one to the other for a moment. Then she burst into laughter—peal after peal of contagious merriment rang through the narrow confines of the *Meteor*. The ice was broken.

Indicating her own person with a sweeping gesture and a bow, the girl uttered a single word, "Lola."

Gary completed the introduction by naming his two friends and himself. The three derived much amusement from her efforts at reproducing his pronunciation of Eddie and Gary. With the single syllable, Ray, she had no difficulty.

The men removed their cumbersome suits and she proceeded to do likewise. When she was revealed in a snugly fitting, silver-hued garment that would have created a furor on one of their bathing beaches at home, they exchanged embarrassed glances. But the girl seemed entirely at ease and unabashed.

It was soon evident that Lola was an extremely intelligent girl, for she immediately realized that explanations could be made only by signs and drawings. She pointed to a wall chart of the Earth and nodded brightly to show that she knew what it represented. By going through the motions of sketching she indicated that she desired to be supplied with drawing materials, and she exclaimed delightedly when Ray handed her a pad of paper and a pencil. She examined both as if they were somewhat strange to her, but after experimenting with the pencil a bit, she started drawing a series of concentric circles on the paper. In the center she drew a small circle, which she speedily shaded to represent a sphere. Then on each of the concentric circles she placed another sphere of smaller size.

"By George!" exclaimed Ray. "She's drawing the solar system."

This was confirmed at once by Lola, who pointed again to the wall chart, then to the sphere on the third concentric circle she had drawn.

"Tora," she averred confidently. Then hesitatingly, "Ray, Ed-dee, Gair-ree-meer Tora."

"She knows we are from the Earth," gasped Ray, "and her name for our planet is Tora."

Lola then pointed to the sphere on her fifth concentric circle and rapidly marked nine small dots at varying distances from this globe.

"The nine satellites of Jupiter!" exclaimed Ray.

She pointed to the fifth dot from the sphere, then to herself, intoning solemnly, "Lola-meer Thares."

"Callisto," said Ray, "the satellite of more than three thousand miles diameter whose distance from Jupiter is one and a third million miles. The girl is from Callisto, or Thares, as she calls it."

"But," objected Gary, "she seems to be at home in our Earth gravity as simulated in the *Meteor*—she was able to leap twenty or more feet on the moon's surface. How can that be if the satellite she hails from is so much smaller than our Earth?"

"The smaller body might still have a similar surface gravity," Ray explained. "Since the kinship of gravity and magnetism was proved, our older estimates based on the mass of a body have been thrown into the discard in many instances. It may well be that this satellite has a gravity equivalent to our own."

Seeing that her efforts were bringing understanding, she tore the first sheet from the pad and started sketching on the second sheet. This girl from the distant satellite was an artist. By the use of a very few strokes she was able to produce wonderful likenesses of human beings, machines, buildings. She first drew a king seated on a throne; then his consort, a beautiful woman. At their feet she drew a child—a girl of perhaps ten years of age whom she called Lola. Their visitor was a princess! She studied their faces and beheld astonished comprehension.

Then she drew even more rapidly, using sheet after sheet of the paper as she warmed to the task. Her sketches formed a picture history of her own life and of the peoples of her own world. She pictured scientific advances made by two separate and distinct races of beings, the one clan being dark-haired like herself—the other seemingly of larger stature and extremely blond. The overthrow of the government and the assassination of her parents she wept over. The plans of the light-haired ones she pictured vividly, showing that their astronomers were cognizant of the desirability of the Earth as a field for conquest. She sketched spaceships of huge size with which the journey was to be made and indicated the plans for using the Earth's satellite as a base for hostile operations. Her own kidnapping by the leader of the warlike blond horde she stormed over, finally ending the story with her escape and subsequent release from her tormentors by the Earthmen.

When she had finished, she turned a happy face to the three men who had watched so silently and admiringly.

"Well, I'll be hornswaggled!" said Eddie. "There's the whole story for us. These doggoned Calisthenics; or whatever you want to call them, are figuring on busting us up back home. Can you beat that for nerve?"

Ray and Gary grinned at his explosive remarks and the silvery laugh of Lola once more brightened the interior of the *Meteor* when she observed the comical expression of consternation that spread over the chubby face of the mechanic.

"All the same," said Ray, "this is a serious matter and I am going to try and learn more from Lola, though I am afraid my own efforts at picture-writing will not be as successful. Meanwhile I think we should repair the landing gear and disarm the helpless Callistonians outside before we release them."

"Right, Chief," said Eddie. "I'll get out the welding outfit and take care of it right away."

He soon had the apparatus ready and again drew on his airtight suit. Before he clamped the helmet in place he cast an admiring look at the sleek blackness of Lola's close-cropped tresses, where she bent over Ray's initial attempt at imitating her method of communicating by means of pictures.

But Ray's efforts proved successful, due to the keen perception of the girl and to occasional help from Gary.

They learned that the lunar base had been in existence only a short time, less than one revolution of the Earth about the sun. Lola's eyes glowed at the pictures of peace, prosperity, and happiness on Earth that Ray did his best to represent. She signified her joy at being within the *Meteor* and her wish to return to the Earth with them. It developed that nearly two years were to be required in which to complete the fleet of spaceships and to establish the lunar base of operation.

Ray indicated his intention of returning to the Earth and preparing its peoples for the warfare to come, even suggesting the possibility of building a fleet of their own to visit first the moon, then the satellite Callisto, destroying the base and then carrying the war to her own world with the express intention of overthrowing the power of the light-haired ones and restoring Lola's own loved ones to their birthright of freedom and happiness. His proposals met enthusiastic approval and by the time Eddie returned with an armful of the enemy's ray projectors, a complete understanding had been reached.

"All fixed, Chief," said Eddie, when he had removed his helmet and pushed the slender weapons under one of the bunks. "The wheel was not damaged. Neither was the axle. They had only burnt off one of the struts and that was easy. It's as good as new now."

"Fine. And now we'll release those poor devils out there."

He pulled the switch that controlled the energy used to overcome them. Lola did not realize the meaning of this action, but when the men glued their eyes to the windows and watched the prostrate figures of the enemies, she knew that the strange instrument in the *Meteor* had something to do with their condition. When one of them commenced moving about and eventually sat upright, she registered a vigorous protest, and there was no misunderstanding the warning note in her voice, though—the words were unintelligible. She hastened to employ the sketchpad once more, but before she was able to bring her talent to further use, there came a surprised cry from Eddie.

"Holy smoke!" he exclaimed. "Here comes a tank!"

An armored caterpillar tractor was bearing down on them from the direction of the village, and most of the recently helpless Callistonians were now on their feet and hailing the approaching war machine with joyful leaps and wavings of the arms. As the monster engine neared them, a ray of shimmering yellow shot forth from its fore part and impinged on the hull of the *Meteor.*

Lola screamed as the vessel was surrounded by impenetrable darkness, but Ray reassured her smilingly. He was confident of the efficacy of the *Meteor's* insulating envelope. But he decided to get out of range of the ray on account of the possibility of it causing damage to the outer structure, so he advanced to the rocket control keyboard and pressed a few of the buttons.

There was no response! And the temperature in the *Meteor* was rising rapidly!

CHAPTER EIGHT
A Callistonian Sphere

"WHAT sort of a bombardment is this?" asked Ray in astonishment. "These must be vibrations of a sort I have never encountered. Our electrical system is paralyzed."

He worked frantically with the keys, but to no avail. The darkness persisted and the temperature continued to rise, though the refrigerating system was working to capacity. He pondered for a moment as Gary and Eddie attempted to calm the now greatly perturbed Lola. She was endeavoring to convey a message to them, but in the excitement of the moment was unable to do so.

"I have it!" Ray suddenly shouted. "Quick, Eddie—the emergency lights! We'll fire the rockets with their batteries."

They hastily dismantled the battery boxes of two of the equipments that had been included in the accoutrements of the *Meteor* on the chance of exploring dark caverns during the visit. They soon had two sets of powerful dry cells and quickly set about tearing at the molding in which were hidden the ignition wires of the rocket tubes. Perspiration poured from their skin as the heat increased, but they worked with unabated energy. Finally the proper wires were located and small sections of insulation were stripped from the copper.

"Now," breathed Ray, "when I give the word, make contact with the battery terminals. Just two short taps on the binding posts. Ready?"

"Ready, Chief," panted Eddie.

Lola and Gary had sunk to their seats, gasping painfully in the superheated atmosphere.

"Now!" said Ray, whose throat was so dry he could scarcely speak.

There were a number of answering raps from below and the two men collapsed where they crouched. The *Meteor* sped from its position with tremendous velocity and was instantly in the glare of the sun. Brilliant beams of its light streamed through the circular windows, as the vessel rose far from the moon's surface, but there were none to observe the cheering sight. Lola and the three men had lost consciousness. But the pumps in the rear compartment continued their whirring and the temperature dropped rapidly. Luckily the refrigerating system was operated from tanks of compressed air and had not ceased functioning when the electrical system was paralyzed by the baleful ray of the Callistonians.

Eddie was first to recover and he stared about him wonderingly as he sat up. For a minute he ruminated dazedly, then he remembered and quickly sprang to his feet.

"Oh, boy!" he drawled, "was that a close one? Another minute and the *Meteor* would have been a fine cemetery."

He rushed to the side of Lola and rubbed her wrists frantically. So marble-white was her skin that he feared she was dead. But he soon whooped his relief as her eyelids fluttered and she drew a long, tremulous breath. Ray and Gary recovered at about the same time.

"Well," said Ray, when he was able to speak, "that was one I didn't count on. And we got out just in time—no question of that."

He looked through the lower windows and observed that they were fully five hundred miles from the moon.

"But we have a ray of our own," he continued grimly, "and I'm going back and I'll give them a dose of their own medicine."

An experimental touch on the keyboard showed that the connections were once more functioning. He pressed several of the keys and they dropped rapidly as the rat-tat of the rocket charges answered. Lola objected strenuously as she saw the ill-omened satellite rushing upward to meet them. She wanted never to return to the place of her most recent sufferings. But Eddie's good-natured smile and assured manner soon reconciled her.

The *Meteor* dropped to within a few hundred feet of its recent position and they were astonished to see that the war machine of the Callistonians had been overturned by the blast from their own rocket tubes. Eddie loaded the camera and made a few more exposures.

Half buried in the powdery footing there were the bodies of a number of the helmeted Callistonians who had been slain in the sudden hurricane resulting from the escape of the *Meteor*. The state of collapse of their garments told of the reason for their passing. The force of the concussion had torn the airtight coverings, allowing the oxygen to escape from within and thus, suffocating the victims. Not an enemy was in sight and Ray headed for their village. Again he was warned by Lola, but he circled the settlement, looking for signs of life. The girl was extremely nervous and they had not long to wait for the reason for her fear. From a number of the cylindrical structures there shot forth duplicates of the ray that had nearly proved their undoing. But the *Meteor* darted hither and thither as Ray manipulated the control keys and it was impossible for the enemy to keep them in range for a long enough time to produce any effect.

Then there came a surprise, for the *Meteor* halted in her rapid movements and was drawn upward by a new and irresistible force. At a quick glance through one of the top windows, Lola cried out in fresh alarm. She had indicated that none of the spaceships from Callisto were on the Earth's satellite. But one had evidently returned in time to witness the maneuverings of the *Meteor*, for high above them hovered a gigantic sphere of polished metal from which depended two large discs like the electromagnets used in the electric cranes on Earth. From these it was apparent the force emanated which was drawing them helplessly aloft.

"Fine kettle of fish!" yelped Eddie. "What to do?"

"We'll try the high-frequency beam on them," replied Ray, leaving the controls.

Lola sat quietly by, an expression of resigned expectation of calamity on her beautiful features.

They started the generators as the rapidity of rise increased and soon the powerful vibrations of the fusing beam were searching the vitals of the great sphere above them. But there was no immediate result and in less than a minute they were thrown to the floor by the heavy jar of striking against the metal discs. They were firmly attached and the discs immediately commenced drawing upward as the cables attached to them were reeled in from above. They were to be brought very close for destruction.

Lola hid her face in despair.

"Can't seem to find a vital spot," grunted Ray, "or else the ship is insulated as we are. But we should be able to fuse away some of the outer covering."

He continued the exploring as a party of helmeted Callistonians dropped from a hatch to the upper surface of the *Meteor.* Their clumsy metal shoes produced a noisy tattoo as they moved about with a heavy piece of machinery which they set up amidships of the top surface of the hull.

"They are about to drill through," groaned Gary.

"Don't worry," said Ray, "we'll stop that."

He started the other transmitter and the vibrations that had overcome the attackers on the surface were at work above. Still he continued with the searching motion of the fusing beam. The sounds above were stilled and they soon heard a body fall to the curved surface, then another and another. Two of the stricken Callistonians slid past a window and slithered over the side, to fall to their death in the village far underneath. Then one of the attracting discs let go and the *Meteor* dropped to an almost perpendicular position, throwing the occupants into a heap against the front partition.

"Got one of their generators!" exulted Ray, crawling back to his beam controls. "Now for the other."

"Yes, and all those birds that were on top are gone," gloated Eddie.

But the weaving beam failed to produce results and Ray finally concentrated it on a protuberance of the immense vessel to which they were attached. There was an almost immediate effect, a small opening fusing through the metal and quickly spreading until a large section of the protuberance had melted and dripped into the depths beneath. There came a quick jerk and the moon's surface receded rapidly as the pilot of the enemy vessel attempted a retreat, not thinking to cast off the barnacle that was causing the damage. And the unwieldy sphere was speedy, for they were soon at a tremendous distance from the previous position. A gaping hole now appeared where the protuberance had existed and the occupants of the *Meteor* knew that the air was escaping from the monstrous vessel above.

Then there was another jerk and the motion of the larger vessel changed to a wobbly, reeling progression that betokened disaster. Apparently its crew had been suffocated and the machinery was out of control. The *Meteor* was doomed to go hurtling through space, an unwilling dangler from the unpiloted vagabond of space!

Ray tried a terrific rocket blast without effect. The energy that had trapped them was too powerful to be thus overcome. Then he experimented with various keys and the direction levers until, with a continuous blast from a single tube, he had swung the *Meteor* about until it lay alongside the spherical hull of the larger ship and he could obtain a view of the supports and feeders of the attracting disc. The fusing beam was then concentrated on the cable fastenings and in a moment they were free, the *Meteor* roaring away from the wandering sphere under the impulses from the single rocket.

"That's that," said Ray, wiping the perspiration from his brow. "I think we had better start for home now before something else happens."

"You said it," agreed Eddie enthusiastically.

Lola trilled her happiness when their intentions were made known to her. And Gary was far from sorry.

CHAPTER NINE
The Meteor Plans a Return

WITH the shadowed side of the moon behind them and the shining greenish orb that was the Earth ahead, Gary conversed seriously with Ray, who was at the controls.

"I fear this presages a fearful conflict," he said. "The radio of the Callistonians has probably advised their home body of the happenings of the past few hours. Should we not have destroyed their lunar headquarters?"

"Probably. But I hated to do it in cold blood. Besides, we can always return in a few hours and I would rather have authority from the government to proceed before engaging in such wholesale slaughter. When we have presented our evidence and have told our story, there must be a conference of the nations. Immediate steps must be taken to prepare adequate defense. Possibly an expedition should be sent to Callisto to fight the war there, as we suggested to Lola."

"It would save our Earth much damage and suffering if we're able to prepare in time. But, with the procrastination and dallying usually indulged in when international questions are under dispute, I have little hope of speedy results being obtained. Do you think our story will be taken seriously?"

"They must believe us. We have supplemented the evidence of the radio messages with an elaborate series of photographs. These should prove conclusive."

Gary frowned dubiously. "But the war itself," he said, "will be an extremely formidable undertaking. How do you think it would be handled most advantageously?"

"My proposal will be to construct a fleet of ships similar to the *Meteor,* but of considerably larger size and equipped with more powerful weapons of offense. Our fusing ray was of insufficient potency, but it will be a simple matter to construct similar apparatus of many times the strength of ours. I will recommend that no less than a hundred of these vessels be built, some in our own country and some in the workshops of France, Germany, England, and the other nations. By dividing the job in this manner it should be possible to have all available in six months or so, provided work can be started at once. With such a fleet properly manned, a very short period of training will suffice and, if the enemy have not anticipated us, the armada can set out for Callisto, stopping en route to destroy their lunar base of operations."

"Sounds reasonable, Ray. I have an idea also that we may be able to decode the Callistonian radio messages with the help of Lola. With that brain of hers she should be able to pick up our language very quickly, and even if she is not familiar with their dot-and-dash code she will be able to teach her own language to some of our linguists who can, in turn, collaborate with the experts of our Secret Service in solving the code. We will thus be in a position to learn of the plans of the enemy in advance."

"Good idea. This is going to be a whole lot of fun—for me at least. And I am sure it will be for you as well."

"It certainly will be. I am looking forward with much interest to the possible deciphering of the enemy messages. But it seems to me the biggest job of all will be to convince our world of the danger that threatens and to obtain official action before it is too late. Think of the calamity that hangs over the heads of our people! Less than a dozen of those huge spheres could lay waste to half of our own United States in a very few days if they struck in our present defenseless condition. I am much concerned over the outlook, having had some experience in getting governmental recognition and action on important matters."

Ray laughed. "I know how you feel, old man," he said. "I have had one or two such experiences myself. But in this case I think there will not be much trouble. The messages—the photographs—the captured weapons of the Callistonians—all are very definite proof of our story. Then we have Lola to present in person."

Gary looked over his shoulder and saw that Lola and Eddie were bent over the pad, on which the girl was again sketching. Ray's eyes followed his friend's glance and a broad grin spread over his features.

"I should have said that Eddie has her to present," he remarked.

The two scientists gazed benignantly at the lovers, whose heads were drawn so close and who seemed so entirely oblivious of their presence in the vessel.

The *Meteor* rushed onward toward the world that was to be rudely awakened to the necessity of arming against a foe from out of space. Unheeding, Lola and Eddie strove desperately to tell each other what was in their minds. The girl, flushed with happiness, suddenly threw her arms about the neck of the man at her side and Ray and Gary turned to stare intently into the screen of the periscope. Each was convulsed with pleased merriment, but they made not a sound.

Eddie found that he could make himself much better understood by the use of caresses than he had been able to do with the sketchpad.

PART TWO

"Callisto at War"

CHAPTER TEN
Return from the Moon

THE Callistonian maiden, Lola, eagerly scanned the beautiful countryside over which the *Meteor* sped when it reached the Earth after its return voyage from the other side of the moon. She thought wistfully of her own home where the foliage was as beautiful as that of the Earth if of slightly different color and appearance; thought of the depredations of the blond giants, who had brought about the overthrow of her own people and the death of their king and queen, her parents. Shudderingly she recalled the obnoxious attentions of the light-haired leader of the last expedition from her own world to the satellite of the one she was now to visit. But she gave thanks as she remembered the brave actions of the three Earthmen who had rescued her from the malevolent chief in that fortress on the desolate globe that was the Earth's moon. And when she turned her pretty head from the window through which she was looking, she cast affectionate glances at the chubby figure of Eddie Dowling, as he bent so intently over the chart upon which their course was plotted.

Eddie and his employer, Ray Parsons, were navigating the tiny vessel, which had ventured outside of the Earth's atmosphere and made the hitherto unaccomplished trip to the moon. Gary Walton, friend and coworker of Ray, lay asleep in one of the bunks, re-living in his dreams those strange adventures, in which they had become involved on the side of the moon not visible from the Earth.

The rocket tubes of the *Meteor* were long since cooled off and the steady purr of the motor in the nose of the ship had taken the place of their intermittent rat-tat, the sound that had assailed the ears of the occupants during the past ten hours. Beneath them in swift succession, there slipped the towns and villages of Connecticut and soon they had passed over the city of New Haven and were following the Boston Post Road, a broad highway black with surface traffic. It was now necessary to reduce the speed of the *Meteor* for they had entered one of the regular air lanes and it was dangerous to exceed the standard speed of two hundred miles an hour as established for the lower levels. In a very few minutes now their journey would be over.

Soon they left the highway and crossed the state line, cutting due west into New York State. When the *Meteor* started circling for a landing in its own enclosure, Lola gurgled with delight. She was to set foot on Tora, the world of peace and prosperity.

With the landing of the craft Gary awoke from his nap and was amazed to learn that he had slept for more than four hours.

Eddie hastened to the air lock and unbolted the outer door, as rapidly as his fingers could manipulate the clamping bolts. All three men were tired, though Gary had been somewhat refreshed by his short sleep. Lola was as fresh as a daisy and could scarcely restrain herself in her eagerness to set foot on the soil of the world of her rescuers.

"What on Earth are we going to do with Lola?" asked Ray, as the door swung outward and Eddie prepared to assist her to the ground.

"You just leave that to me now, Chief," was the eager reply. "My house is just a couple of miles down the road as you know, and my mother and sister will welcome her with open arms."

Gary grinned as Lola jumped from the opening into the waiting arms of Eddie, who had preceded them. "And that is about the way you seem to be welcoming her too," he said.

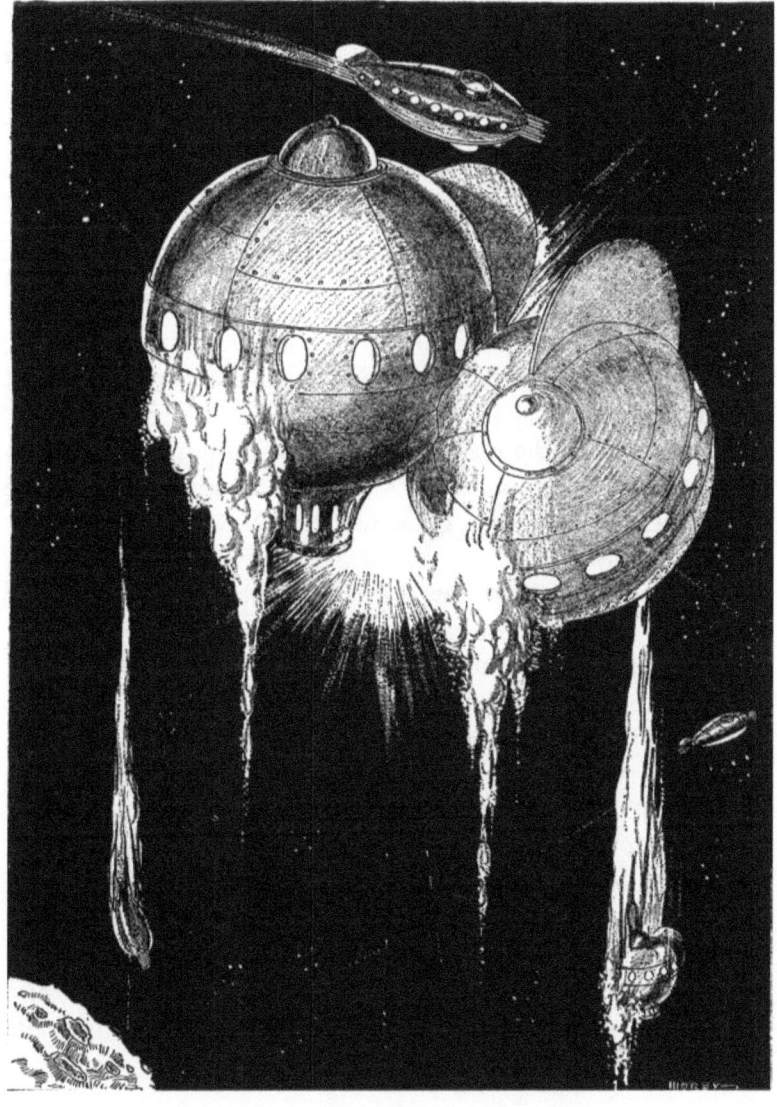

The smiling mechanic flushed to the roots of his hair but was at no loss for a reply. "You bet your life," he averred, "and, believe me, I'm going to hang onto this little girl, if I have to call out the marines to help."

"I'm afraid she will be a very busy little person," countered Ray, who was the last to step from the shiny craft. "You know we are depending upon her to do a great deal in getting this stupendous story across to our people and convincing them that immediate action is necessary for defense against the blond Callistonians."

Lola stood at one side, gazing about expectantly but seeing nothing except the grassy field and the high fence surrounding it. She realized that the men were discussing her, but felt secure in the belief that whatever they decided would be for her good.

"Anyway," Eddie maintained stoutly, "you are all going to stay at my house tonight. It's too late to do anything more today and we all need a good night's rest. Lots of room at our house too."

"You win," laughed Ray. "The invitation is accepted. But I'm not so sure that your mother will be pleased."

"Sure she will!" And Eddie hastened to the door of the enclosure to get out one of the cars.

Ray and Gary exchanged amused glances as Lola followed, almost on the heels of the exuberant mechanic. But they had grave misgivings as they surveyed the scantily clothed figure of the dark haired maiden. She was entirely too pretty and the silver hued garment entirely too snug and sparse to meet with the approval of a matron of the caliber of Eddie's mother. But it seemed that there was nothing to do but to comply with Eddie's wishes, so they trailed in his wake and were soon ensconced in the rear seat of his ancient gasoline motored car.

When they stepped from the car at the door of Eddie's modest home, Mrs. Dowling rushed across the porch to meet them.

"Sakes alive, Edward Dowling," she said, "where you been?"

Then she stopped aghast at the vision of the radiant girl, whose silver garment glistened in the light of the setting sun with a thousand shimmering hues.

"And bringin' one of them bathin' beauties home with you too!" she continued indignantly.

But when Lola advanced toward her, face wreathed in the sweetest of smiles, she extended her hands. Then, looking deep into the eyes of this girl from another world, she suddenly threw her arms about the slim figure and drew the dark head to her motherly bosom.

CHAPTER ELEVEN
Each to His Own Task

THE following day was a bewildering one for Lola, and for Eddie a day of acute misery. For, with their minds alert to the extreme seriousness of the situation, Ray and Gary took things into their hands immediately following the morning meal in the Dowling home. Lucky it was that Eddie's sister took an immediate liking to the girl from Callisto; lucky also that the two were of about the same build, thus making it possible for the Earth-girl to provide suitable dress for the young lady who was about to set out on the mission of warning and assisting a world that was in grave danger.

At a hurry call from Gary, the president of the International Communications Corporation dispatched his private airplane to carry Lola to the headquarters of the Company in New York City. It seemed to Eddie that no plane had ever traveled so swiftly as that one, and when Lola was hustled inside and whisked away from his sight, his usually smiling countenance took on such an expression of gloom that his mother identified the symptoms at once. But she was wise enough to say nothing, for she knew that her boy must be about his business. It was Eddie who must superintend the overhauling of the *Meteor* for its next voyage. Besides, she was not overly anxious to lose him and certainly this little girl from somewhere out there in the sky seemed quite capable of taking him away.

Lola's impressions of the succeeding few hours were so confused that she could not well have described her experiences, had she been called upon to do so by one who spoke her language. The swift rush to the great city whose entire upper surface seemed to be one huge landing space for aircraft—the rapid descent into a great, magnificent room where a kindly faced Earthman patted her hand, while Ray and Gair-ree spoke rapidly to him in their own peculiar language—the subsequent facing of great blinding lights, where many Earth men spoke rapidly before huge numbers of black boxes, and where she was paraded before a succession of mirrors that reflected her own image in the strange costume that was so encumbering—all was so unfamiliar that she did not understand any of it.

But these Earth people were so kind and so solicitous that she loved them all, and she sensed that the strange proceedings were entirely in the interest of the plan mentioned by Ray, on the journey from Earth's satellite. And with every fiber of her tender being she was glad—glad that these people were taking measures in their own defense, and hopeful of the result of this action being beneficial to her own race as well. She could not help but observe the intense energy with which the Earth folk attacked their problems and the efficiency of their labors.

With the completion of the ordeal of what she later learned was her official presentation over the world news-broadcast, she thought that her duties were completed for a time. But Lola was to be given very little rest, and she soon found herself in another fast airplane crossing a considerable body of water. At her side was the kindly Earthman with the gray hair. This was Horace Greenfield, President of the International Communications Corporation. There were also in the plane two of the men who had rescued her, Ray and Gary. But Eddie had been left behind.

"Gary," said Greenfield, "the effect of the announcements has been tremendous. Before we left New York anxious communications were coming through from all over the world. It was fortunate indeed that the equipment of the *Meteor* included developing tanks and enlarging apparatus, so that you were able to show the pictures along with the verbal report. And the final showing of Miss Lola was a staggering climax."

"Yes, that's true, Mr. Greenfield. And we must thank Ray Parsons for his foresight in so thoroughly equipping his vessel. But I still fear very much for the success of our venture in attempting to get the nations of the world sufficiently interested in this thing to make the preparations we believe are necessary."

"I would not fear for that, Gary. President Cobham, as you know, is a personal friend of mine. We were boys together. And his influence in the present administration is such that Congress dares not oppose him on any important matters. Once the thing is put across in our own country the other nations are bound to follow suit."

"But," interrupted Ray, "there is much to be done. We must first arrange for Lola's session with the telepathists and linguists, so that she will be quickly able to assist in decoding the messages from the lunar base of the enemy. This is by far the surest and quickest means of assuring immediate action in preparation for the war that is bound to come very soon now. I say soon now on account of the recent developments up there on the moon."

"That too shall be taken care of," replied Greenfield. "In all departments of the government I have considerable influence and no stone will remain unturned when we reach Washington. Lola shall be taken in hand immediately."

"Poor kid," mused Ray, stealing a glance at the girl who gazed interestedly from the window at her side. "She doesn't know what it is all about, but she trusts us as if she had known us all her life."

"Yes, but she is going to be far happier than she has been in several years when this is all over. And I tell you, young man that the biggest share of the preparation is going to fall on your shoulders. Our world has forgotten the arts of warfare and it seems to me that even the weapons with which you armed the *Meteor* are insufficient to cope with this enemy if it comes to a conflict of great scope, as this will undoubtedly be. As our foremost inventor, you will be confronted with the task of devising adequate armament for the vessels that we are to request the governments of the world to construct."

Ray looked grave. "Yes I suppose that's true, Mr. Greenfield," he admitted, "and it is a task that will require my immediate and whole-hearted attention. But we shall succeed, never fear."

"No doubt of that whatever," came the hearty response. He turned once more to Gary. "And, you my boy," he continued, "must carry on the work of keeping in touch with these code messages and must see to it that the world is kept advised of developments as quickly as we are able to decipher them with the aid of this girl from Callisto."

Gary seemed crestfallen. "But—but, Mr. Greenfield," he objected, "I had hoped to be able to collaborate with Ray here on the more important work."

"Tut, tut, Gary. Every man to his own line. And to my way of thinking the communications end of this problem is every bit as important as any other. Mark my words; that phase of the matter is going to provide the key to the entire situation."

They were approaching Washington and Lola exclaimed with delight at the beauty of the city that spread beneath them. Certainly in the march of progress, it alone of all American cities had retained its beauty, cleanliness, and charm. And, when they landed before the Capitol, it seemed that the entire city had turned out to welcome them.

Lola breathed deeply with excitement when she observed the great throngs about the square and she could have thrown herself into the arms of the kindly little gray-haired woman who greeted her at the side of President Cobham, though she knew not that this was the first lady of the land or that her consort was its chief executive.

CHAPTER TWELVE
Preparing for Defense

THEN came many days of grueling activity for all members of the party, which had so short a time ago returned from the moon. To Lola the succeeding events were of such intense interest that she promptly forgot all else; forgot the problems of her own people; forgot poor Eddie. But within six days, thanks to the ceaseless efforts of telepathists and linguists, she was able to converse in English and several of the students had mastered the two tongues of her own Callisto. All who came in contact with the Callistonian maiden were charmed, and it was rumored about official

Washington that Eugene Cobham, only son of the president, was desperately in love with her.

Ray had returned to his own laboratory and was resolutely striving to contrive weapons of defense and offense that would be capable of decisively overwhelming the enemy with whom he knew they must deal. In this work he was assisted by his own staff of workmen, including the now changed and morose Eddie Dowling. Eddie had heard some of the rumors that were being circulated in Washington and his rotundity seemed to become less and less apparent as the days passed. More than that, his usual smile was seen no more, but that was not so noticeable, for all the Parsons workmen were working under extreme pressure and there was little time for jocoseness. Ray himself was in unusually bad humor, for the first experiments had come to naught.

Gary organized a special force to classify the tape messages received from the lunar transmitter of the Callistonians and when the Secret Service experts arrived at his office with complete data on the two languages of Callisto, he was ready for them. The labor of working out the code was commenced at once and within ten days this was completed, though it proved to be a stupendous task. Day by day the operatives became more expert and it was soon possible to have the messages decoded, translated, and ready for the news broadcasts within one hour after their reception.

A conference of the nations was in progress in Washington and, with the passage of time an agreement was reached and work was begun. At this stage of the proceedings Ray Parsons was called to Washington and there he spent many days in conference with the foremost aviation experts of the world, drawing plans for the war vessels that were to be constructed. Of course, appropriations had been cut to the bone, so that by the time the diplomats were finished with the plans, the number of vessels to be built had dwindled to a mere thirty, ten of which were to be constructed in the United States. Ray shrugged his shoulders at this news but resolved that the thirty ships should be so well-armed as to prove a match for any fleet the blond Callistonians might be able to muster. But when he finished with the other designers and the plans of the new war ships were completed, he was no nearer the solution of the armament problem than he had been previously. True, the new ships were to be provided with the various energies used by the *Meteor* and the generators of the energies were to be of far greater power. But a real, invincible weapon was still to be discovered.

All over the world industry was drafted for the work of turning out the thirty vessels in the shortest possible time. In this influence of Horace Greenfield predominated. It was he who organized the financiers of the world and laid down the law to them. It was his influence with President Cobham that brought about the various conferences in which international agreements were ratified, and it was he who kept the news broadcasts constantly filled with the right sort of propaganda. The messages from the moon played no small part, for each day revealed a new development in the plot of the enemies of the world. Excitement prevailed throughout the globe as it became apparent that a preliminary sortie was being planned by the enemy.

Before Ray left Washington to return to his own laboratory, he attempted to visit Lola but was extremely disappointed on learning that she was too busily engaged with social functions to grant him an audience. And the rumors concerning Eugene Cobham persisted. But at least he would not apprise Eddie of this fact. That would be entirely too much of a blow at the present time, he thought.

Upon his return to the laboratories in Monroe County he was surprised at finding Gary awaiting his arrival.

"Just took a couple of days off," was his friend's greeting. "Old Greenfield thinks I need a rest and I thought I'd come up here and pal around with you a bit. Heard you were leaving Washington today so I beat you to it in getting here."

"Glad to see you, old man," replied Ray wearily but earnestly, "but I'm afraid you won't get much rest. This question of armament must be settled pronto so I'll be working day and night. Of course that doesn't mean you have to be on the job, but knowing you as I do, I'm darn sure you will be, whether I want you to or not."

"Right," grinned Gary, "and that's just what I want. I'm so sick of looking at the tapes and listening to the translators that I could fly. The change will be the rest I need. How's Lola?"

"Hush." Ray looked to see if Eddie was within hearing. "The darn kid's had her head turned with all the fuss they've been making over her and it's pretty sure she's running around with young Cobham quite steadily. Mustn't let Eddie know, but she wouldn't even see me."

"Fiddlesticks! That girl's head is never going to be turned. She's too smart. The only trouble is that they have been rushing her so that doesn't know what to do about it. Don't forget that all of this is entirely new to her. She'll get over it."

"Hope so. Anyhow, what do you say we quit gabbing and get to work on this armament business?"

"Right."

So the two friends once more started work on a knotty problem and when Eddie Dowling offered his services in the particular work, Ray dismissed him rather curtly and ordered him to complete the overhauling of the *Meteor* and the restocking of the ship for a much longer voyage. He turned his head resolutely from the hurt look in Eddie's eyes.

"Whew! Glad that's over," he exclaimed, when the crestfallen mechanic left them. "Poor old Eddie is eating his heart out over Lola and I just can't stand it to watch him. Besides I think we are going to need the old *Meteor* on this job."

"What? You think she can make the trip to Callisto?"

"Why not? We don't have to carry any more of the concentrate than we did on the trip to old Luna and as far as Parsonite goes, she carries enough to send her to the edge of the solar system and bring her back too. Of course there is the question of increased speed, but that is being taken care of now."

"The new ships will be faster?"

"Nearly a hundred times as speedy, Gary."

"A hundred times! Is that possible? Is it necessary?"

"It is easily possible. I have merely redesigned the rocket tubes to provide the proper expansion ratio on which I previously erred. There will be a greater number of tubes also—in fact, we are adding six to the *Meteor*. And the increased speed is of vital importance, unless we want to spend a year or more in making the trip to Callisto."

"Great Caesar's ghost! Is it that far?"

"You bet. Jupiter is 483 million miles from the sun, and the satellite Callisto is one and one-sixth million miles from its parent body. The Earth is but 93 million miles from the sun, and our own moon, which we recently visited, is a little less than a quarter of a million miles from us. So you can see the ratio of distances. Even with Earth and Jupiter in their present positions with relation to the sun, which is nearly as close as the two planets approach each other, the distance is well over 400 million miles and a speed of something like seventy thousands miles a minute for the entire trip average will be required to reach our destination in four days. That is the mark I am shooting at and I have calculated a maximum speed for the new vessels and the remodeled *Meteor* of better than a hundred thousand miles a minute, with a practical cruising speed of eighty-five thousand."

"Wow! That's going some!"

"It is that. But we'll need all the speed we can get, to my way of thinking, when things start popping."

"Are the new ships to be constructed along the same lines as the *Meteor?*"

"Pretty much, with the exception that their wings, landing gears and propellers, which are used only for flying under atmospheric conditions, will be so arranged that they may be folded out of sight and completely protected within the insulated hull. That will prevent these parts being destroyed during an engagement with the enemy. In addition the new ships will Le much larger than the *Meteor.* But here—this talk isn't getting us anywhere on the question of a super-weapon."

CHAPTER THIRTEEN
The Tellurians' Defense in Space

GARY'S so-called vacation stretched into ten days and their labors had produced less than nothing in the way of that invincible weapon for which they were searching. At the end of the ten-day period it was necessary for Gary to return to New York and Ray was at almost his wit's end. He was constantly besieged with urgent radiophone requests from the government for news regarding the results of his investigations. Annoying calls from antagonistic scientists, who sought only to renew some of the old quarrels they had with him, served further to irritate and exasperate him. He shut himself up from all callers after a few experiences of this sort and worked harder than ever. They would not down Ray Parsons!

Meanwhile the thirty vessels were well under way in various parts of the world. Parsonite was being manufactured in huge quantities in order that the rocket tubes of the new ships might be well supplied. The concentrated fuel for the internal combustion engines was likewise being refined in large quantities, and was stored in great tanks that were erected at several shipyards. Oxygen generators, carbon dioxide absorption apparatus, generators of the paralyzing and fusing high frequency currents, and other required portions of the ships were being built with all possible speed and shipped to the yards for installation in the vessels. But still there was no super-armament.

Then came the day when the world was stunned by the news that a fleet of the Callistonian vessels was scheduled to make an experimental raid on the Earth within the next forty-eight hours and Ray's radiophone was kept constantly busy. What are we to do? This was the cry from the four corners of the globe. And, despite the seriousness of the situation, Ray was constrained to make merry over some of the frantic communications from his erstwhile critical colleagues. To each and every inquiry he made the same reply. The fusing and paralyzing ray generators were to be installed in any sort of aircraft that would carry them, and the observatories were to keep constant watch of the heavens for the approach of the attacking ships, when a defense was to be made, with the improvised fleet after the enemy vessels entered the Earth's atmosphere. Secretly he determined that the *Meteor* would be on hand when the time came.

Further messages, when decoded, revealed that the raid was to be made by eight of the huge spheres from Callisto, and that these were already assembled at the lunar base. Fortunately the messages likewise revealed the points of intended attack, so it was a comparatively simple matter for the Tellurians to concentrate their meager armament at the expected localities. But the time was short and the panics that resulted in the various cities where attacks were anticipated resulted in serious privation and considerable loss of life. There was no doubt as to the objectives, for the messages indicated clearly that the largest cities of the several continents were chosen. New York, Chicago, Philadelphia, Paris, London, Berlin, Tokyo, and Osaka were undoubtedly the cities under fire, each to be attacked by a single sphere. The exodus from each of these centers was overwhelming and the authorities could not handle it. Engineers and mechanics labored day and night, transporting the sixteen generating equipments that had been completed, and installing them in the fastest commercial planes that could be requisitioned. There were three at New York, two at each of the other cities excepting Osaka, which was unfortunate in being able to obtain but one.

Early in the morning of the second day the news broadcasts reported that the fleet of eight vessels had been sighted by various observatories and that they were approaching the Earth at a distance of less than one hundred thousand miles. Ray decided that it was time for action and he dropped his work and hurried to the *Meteor*.

"Eddie," he said to the surprised mechanic, "is she ready for the air?"

"Never better Chief. Where to?"

"You heard about the fleet that is coming to attack?"

"Sure, on the broadcast last night. What of it?"

"They have been sighted, and we are going out to meet them."

"Hot stuff! Let's go!" Eddie was himself once more and he bounded through the air lock as if on springs.

Ray grinned delightedly as he clamped the outer door. Good old Eddie, he thought, he'd get over this foolish love affair.

Eddie started the motor and in less than a minute the *Meteor* was roaring out over the treetops and climbing rapidly into the rare air regions. The ship operated without a hitch and seemed to sense that it was being called upon to make an extra effort. The Earth fell away from them. The acceleration compensators were taxed to the limit and Ray felt himself pressed into his seat with painful force. He corrugated his brow in thought. This gravity thing might offer a solution of the armament problem—if he but knew how to adapt it. Then he promptly forgot the glimmering of an idea that had come to him, for he noted that they were traveling at the rate of two thousand miles a minute.

"Ease up there, Eddie," he ordered, "they're only a hundred thousand miles out. We'll overshoot the mark."

With the answering tattoo from the forward rockets and the resulting deceleration, he was lifted from his seat and found difficulty in maintaining his equilibrium. Once more came that hazy forming of an idea, only to be dashed from his mind by a shout from the excited Eddie.

"There they are, Chief! Over to the right!"

It was true and they were rapidly passing the massed fleet of the Callistonians, but at a considerable distance. The *Meteor* had now slowed down considerably and Eddie manipulated the controls to swing the ship about in a wide arc. The stuttering of the explosions in the rocket tubes was almost continuous for a few seconds and then they were on the back trail with the eight spheres of the enemy in formation far ahead and barely visible in the periscope screen. The *Meteor* drew rapidly nearer and Ray started the generators of the fusing beam.

"Now Eddie," he said tensely, "just approach slowly until we are only a few miles to their rear. Then keep that position."

He chose the rearmost of the eight spheres and, when within range, searched its vitals with the destructive ray from the machine at which he stood. For a minute there was no result. Then he recalled the effect previously obtained on one of the protuberances of a similar vessel. He made out the bulge of such a protuberance and directed the ray at this point with immediate effect. The knob-like appendage flattened to the level of the surrounding metal and very quickly a large jagged opening appeared where the deadly beam contacted with the hull.

"One!" exulted Ray. But his triumph was short lived, for the formation of the enemy ships changed at once, two of them dropping out of formation and five increasing their speed in the direction of the Earth, which now appeared as a great, spotted green ball that nearly filled the heavens. The damaged sphere wobbled uncertainly and went reeling off into space. But the two spheres that had fallen behind turned to attack the tiny *Meteor.*

"Now, we are in for it!" grunted Ray. "Keep a close watch on the controls, old man, and I'll tend to this beam."

Eddie needed no further instructions, for when he saw that the two spheres were separating and maneuvering to attack from opposite directions, he shot the *Meteor* to one side so swiftly that she came up under one of the big vessels and gave Ray an opportunity to get in an immediate shot at the lower prominence on the hull. The beam took effect very quickly, but not before that shimmering yellow ray had been released by the enemy vessel. It struck the *Meteor* amidships and, as had happened in the encounter over the surface of the moon, the temperature rose rapidly in their small cabin. Simultaneously the electrical system of the *Meteor* became completely paralyzed and Ray groaned in despair. Meanwhile the second sphere was swinging about to get within reach of the tiny vessel that had attacked its sister ship. Eddie worked frantically with the controls but to no avail. Then, as suddenly as it had appeared, the yellow beam vanished and soon the answering tattoo of the rockets told of the release from the energy it carried. The *Meteor* shot into space with tremendous velocity.

"Another close call, Eddie," shouted Ray as he wiped the perspiration from his face. "Now get the other."

But the second sphere was vanishing rapidly in the direction of the Earth, which suddenly loomed very close. Ray glanced at the distance indicator.

"Good Lord, they've gotten away," he exclaimed. "Only ten thousand miles to go and we can't possibly overtake them in that short distance. Well, we accounted for two of them and the only thing we can do is return to New York and help out there."

So the little *Meteor* was hurled Earthward to enter the battle that must surely have commenced by this time.

CHAPTER FOURTEEN
The World's Largest Cities in Danger

OVER the great city of New York there circled three large steel monoplanes, each powered by six motors of tremendous size. These were the highest speed standard planes obtainable and were capable of traveling at five hundred miles an hour at twenty thousand feet altitude. Each was equipped with a fusing beam generator and was manned by ten picked members of the police force in addition to an expert pilot and two mechanicians. These planes were not insulated like the *Meteor*, so instructions had been issued to fight the battle at as long range as possible in order to keep away from the yellow beam of the invader and from the powerful magnetic energy, concerning which Ray and Gary had reported.

When the gigantic sphere of the Callistonians appeared over the lower portion of the city, its polished surface gleaming in the midday sun, the three defense planes circled faster and faster, climbing rapidly to a point where they were enabled to attack the monster. Seemingly unmindful of its small tormentors, the great sphere sank speedily to a point directly over the Municipal Building, where the yellow ray was put into operation. The tall building crumbled into the surrounding area like a mass of molten paraffin, the white-hot materials flowing along the surrounding streets like lava from a volcanic eruption. Above the spherical vessel the three planes, darting like gnats, tried out their fusing beams on its upper surface. Two more of the yellow rays sprang into action from above and two of the steel ships of the defenders came crashing into the streets, their ignition systems paralyzed and the cabins heated to incandescence. The third, more fortunate than the others, banked sharply and circled the great sphere at so rapid a rate as to make it impossible for the attackers to keep their yellow rays in contact with its steel body. But, by reason of the great speed, it was likewise impossible for the defense plane to get results from its own fusing beam.

It was at this moment that the *Meteor* arrived on the scene and the hitherto hovering sphere rose rapidly to a greater altitude, evidently preferring to battle the new adversary where greater freedom of movement was permissible. The steel plane followed, but was unable to climb as rapidly as the *Meteor,* which darted after the sphere at a speed double that of the Callistonian sphere. Ray struck for the vulnerable lower protuberance with his fusing beam, but was too late. The yellow ray had struck first and the engine of his vessel went dead. Simultaneously the generator of the fusing beam ceased operating and the *Meteor* was helpless under the fire of the enemy vessel. But the insulating hull of the *Meteor* saved them for an instant and this was just sufficient time to permit of the steel plane coming to the rescue. Fortunately the inexperienced operator of the beam aboard the steel plane chanced to direct his energy into the very protuberance, where it was most effective, and the day was saved for New York City. Evidently the controls of the vessel were located in this lower bump, for the great ship immediately commenced its wobbling descent and was soon lost in a cloud of dust which arose upon its crashing into a great section of the east side of lower New York, where all beneath it was demolished.

Then Ray turned on the broadcast receiver of the *Meteor* and picked up the international news service. The world was aghast. The first word to greet them was to the effect that one of the spheres of the invaders had laid waste nearly half of the city of Chicago before departing. Berlin was in flames at a dozen points and its attacker had also left for regions unknown. Paris and London had shared like fates. Tokyo and Osaka escaped entirely, thanks to the destruction of the two spheres outside the Earth's atmosphere. But Philadelphia was still under fire so, with the *Meteor's* motor once more functioning normally, Ray directed Eddie to proceed there with all possible speed. Within fifteen minutes they were circling the smoking ruins of a great section of the third largest city in the United States. Glancing skyward they saw the vanishing bulk of the Callistonian vessel that had so seriously crippled the Quaker City and taken such widespread toll of its population.

"After them, Eddie!" growled Ray. And once more the *Meteor* shot skyward.

But the great sphere was fast and it was many minutes before they approached within range of the fusing beam. Then the most disheartening of all experiences occurred, for the yellow ray of the enemy struck them before their energy could be used and once more the *Meteor* went absolutely dead as far as operation of the electrical equipment was concerned. The enemy had learned how to combat them!

Fortunately for the *Meteor* and its occupants, the enemy ship did not attack. Satisfied that the yellow ray had crippled the small attacking ship, the great sphere proceeded on its swift way toward the lunar base, leaving the *Meteor* to drift helplessly in space until the effects of the bombardment had worn off and the ignition system once more could be used. When the rocket tubes again fired, the spherical vessel had entirely vanished, and Ray ordered Eddie to head for home. Discouraged beyond measure, he closed his eyes and racked his brains for that elusive idea that had been almost within his grasp in the morning. Finally he gave up what was obviously a futile attempt.

When they returned to the laboratory they found a delegation awaiting them, a committee from Washington. Long faces confronted them and Ray's spirits sank to the lowest level they had reached since the beginning of the trouble.

"Gentlemen," he addressed them wearily, "I am fully aware of the reason for your visit, though the details of the disaster to our world are still unknown to me. You have come to me to learn whether I have discovered a super-weapon, have you not?"

"Yes," replied the chairman of the committee, "and it is an extremely serious matter, Mr. Parsons. Perhaps you do not know that our defenses failed in all excepting the one instance, that is, over New York City. And, even here, the steel plane would have failed had it not been that your own ship was occupying all of the attention of the enemy. You witnessed the destruction in Philadelphia, but perhaps you do not know that five other great cities of the world have met a like fate. Our present weapons are inadequate, since even with the new vessels insulated, as is the *Meteor*, we still have no assurance of victory over a superior force. Something must be done immediately."

"Yes I know. But I am no magician, you know. And I must remind you that I want to be left alone and must have absolute quiet if I am to work out our salvation. I shall do my best, but that is all I can promise you. No man can do more."

"We realize that," admitted the chairman, "and we likewise realize that scientists throughout the entire world have been at the same problem, endeavoring to solve it themselves to your discredit. These scientists are still unsuccessful and we have come primarily to assure you that the governments of the world are placing their confidence in you as the one man who can get them out of this unexpected dilemma. We offer every assistance, financial or otherwise, that you may require for your success."

Ray brightened somewhat. "Thank you gentlemen," he said. "I appreciate the honor, as well as the offer of assistance. But my means are entirely sufficient to carry out the work and I have an extremely capable force of assistants. More would simply be in the way and would retard rather than hasten the work. Now, if it please you, will you kindly leave me to my work and carry back to the world the assurance that everything possible will be done. It is not necessary for me to say any more."

The chairman bowed and, after some desultory conversation, the committee left.

"Confound them all!" exclaimed Ray. "Can't they leave a man in peace?"

Then Ray Parsons did an unprecedented thing. He went to bed and, in sheer exhaustion, slept for more than twenty hours.

CHAPTER FIFTEEN
Artificial Gravity

GARY WALTON paced the floor of his office, listening apprehensively to the voice of the news broadcast announcer as the casualty lists were being read. The destruction and loss of life had been of vast extent and the world was in an uproar. Something must be done to speed up the work on the thirty space fliers and to provide adequate means of combating this enemy from out the skies. Worst of all there came widespread criticism of the seeming inactivity of Ray Parsons and of his failure to provide a suitable weapon of offense.

"Fools!" snorted Gary. "Don't they realize that everything that has been done is due to his efforts and that he really saved New York City from the worst disaster of all? Haven't they sense enough to know that except for Ray, we should have been entirely unprepared and that these eight ships would probably have remained here and continued the work of destruction until it was complete? Such ingratitude makes me incensed!"

Then there came from the broadcast receiver a message that had been translated within the past half hour; one of the intercepted messages of the Callistonians. How the enemy gloated! It was true that they had lost two of the eight ships, but they reported that the world was a defenseless one, unprepared and ready for the slaughter. Just one tiny vessel they reported as able to cope with them at all and they bragged that successful means of fighting this lone ship, the *Meteor,* had been discovered. How discouraged Ray must be if he listened to all this rot, thought Gary. And he stamped from his own office to that of Horace Greenfield in high dudgeon.

"I'm resigning, Mr. Greenfield," he stated bluntly, when he faced his superior.

The great executive looked at him with a twinkle in his eyes. "You are, eh?" he countered. "And suppose I refuse to accept your resignation?"

"You must accept it," Gary's tone was stubborn. "I'm all fed up on this communications business at a time like this. I simply can't stand it. If I can't be out doing something worthwhile, I'll go crazy."

"How would you like a leave of absence instead?"

"Oh, that would be great. But I hesitated to ask for it."

"You may have it, my boy, for as long a time as may be necessary. And at full salary too. The work here is so well organized now, that it can go on uninterrupted, and I see no reason why you should not go up there in Monroe County and work with your friend Parsons. I know very well that such a procedure is what has been on your mind."

"That's it, Mr. Greenfield. It galls me to hear all this unwarranted criticism of Ray and I wish to be with him to help in any small way that I can."

"Very natural Gary. Can't say I blame you at all. And now go ahead and run along before I change my mind."

So it was that Gary reached his friend's laboratory within an hour of the time when he awakened from his long sleep. He was astonished beyond measure to find Ray in a great state of excitement, issuing orders right and left among his corps of engineers.

"Just the fellow I wanted to see," Ray greeted him. "You can dig right in and help too. I've solved the problem of a weapon—dreamed it, by George!"

"Dreamed it?"

"Well partly. I had a hazy idea in the formative state, when I fell asleep, but found it fully developed when I awoke. It's a cinch, but we must hurry in order to get the necessary equipment out in time."

"What on earth is this big idea?"

"Come in to my office and I'll tell you all about it. The gang is all primed up now and is going to get busy at once."

They returned to the office and Ray sank into his chair with a contented sigh. Gary was pleased to see that his friend had recovered his usual poise and confidence.

"Artificial gravity," said Ray solemnly, when they had lighted their cigars. "That is the big idea. You know how simply I have been able to increase the force of gravity in the appliances on the *Meteor?*"

"Yes, but how are you to apply that in this case?"

"Listen. It's so simple it's foolish. For years I have been trying to overcome gravity, as have many others of our scientists. But none of us has been successful. However, I have learned how to increase it—how to produce an artificial gravity as is done on the *Meteor*. The acceleration and deceleration compensators operate on the same principle. And the force by which these results are produced can be set up in metallic objects from a distance by means of a definite high frequency current sent over a ray of etheric vibrations. Come over here and I'll show you."

He led his friend to the adjoining room, where there was a huge Coolidge tube and its accompanying apparatus. "Watch this," he said gleefully.

The closing of a switch on a nearby panel lighted the heater element of the tube and Ray adjusted a small reflecting mechanism at the side of the apparatus until a faintly discernible ray of purplish light impinged upon a block of steel, which reposed on a small empty packing case. Nothing happened for a moment and Gary looked questioningly at his friend.

"Wait!" said Ray.

They watched the steel cube in expectant silence. Then something did happen; something so astonishing to Gary that he gasped in amazement. The rough pine boards of which the packing case was constructed sagged lower and lower until, with a sharp crack, they gave way and allowed the steel block to fall to the floor beneath. There was another crash and a thud as of a tremendously heavy object striking the concrete floor of the basement. The cube had gone through and buried itself in the concrete, leaving a gaping opening in the floorboards.

"Great Caesar!" ejaculated Gary, "that's a stunt, old man!"

Ray grinned delightedly at his friend's expression. "Yes," he admitted, "and it is just the stunt that is going to put the Callistonian space fliers out of business."

"But how?"

"Don't you see? That piece of steel, weighing normally about thirty pounds; has been increased in weight by the action of this ray until something like ten or fifteen tons were concentrated on its narrow base and the supports failed. What I propose is that generators of this ray be installed on the *Meteor* and on a few of the larger new ships for use against the enemy vessels. If we encounter them near the surface of the moon or of their own planet it will be possible to send them crashing to the ground. In case we encounter them in space they will crash into each other, due to the greatly increased mutual attraction."

"But will not this increased attraction cause our own ships to crash into those of the enemy as well?"

"No, for the hulls of our vessels are constructed from materials that insulate them against this artificial gravity field. There is no question about it; we have them where we want them now, provided we are in time."

Gary grabbed him by the shoulders and executed an impromptu war dance about him. "Glory be!" he shouted. "You've done it again! And won't the old fossils be sore— the ones who have been knocking you?"

Then there came a startling interruption, for with a pattering rush of tiny feet a slight feminine figure dashed across the room and soft, warm arms were flung around the necks of the two men. It was Lola!

"Oh Ray—oh Gair-ree," she sobbed. "Lola is so unhappy. She has missed her dear friends so much when in the great city you call Wash-ing-ton. Where is Ed-dee?"

Over the top of the girl's head Gary winked at his friend. "What did I tell you?" he said. "Lola is one little bit of all right."

Ray gazed blankly at his friend and at the flushed and panting girl. Where indeed was Eddie? He had not seen him since the last trip of the *Meteor,* since the battle. He rushed to the telephone and soon had Mrs. Dowling on the wire. There was a catch in her voice when she replied to his inquiries.

"My boy has packed his clothes and gone away, Mr. Parsons," she moaned. "Feelin' bad about that Miss Lola, I think he was, and he wouldn't tell me where he was goin' either. It's just sick at heart I am about it, too."

Ray turned from the instrument and faced Lola with a sinking heart. He dared not tell her the truth, yet he knew that she must soon know. So he broke the news as gently as possible.

"Eddie has gone away," he said gravely.

"Gone away?" The girl's eyes were tragic with fear. "Where?"

"We don't know."

Lola dropped weakly into a chair and covered her face with her hands. "Oh, oh," she lamented. "It is that he thought Lola no longer cares. And Lola is to blame. Poor Ed-dee! Unhappy Lola!"

CHAPTER SIXTEEN
A Stowaway

DURING the succeeding weeks the news broadcasts carried different tidings to the peoples of the world. Ray Parsons was once more an international hero. The construction of the thirty vessels was being rapidly rushed to completion. Twelve of the fusing-beam generators intended for the new ships had been destroyed by the raiding party and these were not to be replaced. Instead, the twelve vessels not provided with this equipment were to be armed with the marvelous new weapon developed in the Parsons laboratories. And, by agreement between the governments, Ray Parsons was appointed as commander-in-chief of the fleet.

The intercepted messages of the enemy were read nightly to the listening millions and the plans for a decisive blow and the subjugation and colonization of Earth by the blond giants from Callisto were laid bare even as they developed. The great spherical war ships were assembling at the lunar base for the coming engagement. Fifty of them, there were to be, and fifty more waiting in Callisto to follow up the war vessels with a migration of many thousands of the blond horde to the Earth. It soon became evident that the Tellurian fleet would be ready in ample time to anticipate the date set for the great battle. With this certainty, the world resumed its normal activities and the work of reconstruction started in the several devastated cities.

Ray did not at first take kindly to his appointment, and finally accepted only under the condition that the *Meteor* was to be flagship of the fleet and that his radio orders should issue there from. His laboratory and workshops were beehives of activity and the G-ray generators, as the new apparatus was termed, were turned out in record time and shipped to the yards where the new vessels were nearing completion.

Mrs. Dowling took Lola into her home, though she fought a hard battle with herself before consenting to this. But the girl was so sweet and so obviously fond of her son, that the motherly heart of the older woman could not resist the appeal of this child, whom her son loved. From Eddie there was no news for several weeks, and Lola berated herself incessantly as the cause of his disappearance. But Ray and Gary comforted her with the suggestion that he had, in his disappointment, enlisted amongst the volunteers called for to man the new war ships. Eventually, through a personal call injected into a news broadcast through the influence of Gary, they learned that this was the case. Much of the anxiety of those he had left behind was thus relieved, but due to strict governmental regulations, they were unable to learn the number of the ship to which he was assigned, nor were they permitted to communicate with him, or he with them.

It was evident that the optical instruments of the Callistonians had not revealed to them the activities on Earth in preparation for the coming war, for the messages gave no indication that resistance was expected. The enemy had already won the war in their own estimation.

The alterations to the *Meteor* were completed. Six new rocket tubes were added and the G-ray generator installed. Sufficient fuel and provisions were stowed away in her compartments to permit of a voyage of several weeks' duration. Her acceleration and deceleration compensators were modified to take care of the greatly increased speed. Then came word that the entire fleet was in readiness and Ray was called to Washington for the final conference in which the plan of attack was to be agreed upon. There still remained eight days before the date set by the enemy for their expected offensive.

Three days later the twenty vessels from foreign shipyards had arrived in the United States and were assembled in various flying fields along the eastern seaboard. Ray returned to his laboratory for the *Meteor*. Meanwhile one of his assistant engineers, Marshall Bostwick, had been instructed in the operation of the small vessel and had taken her up for a number of trials. She was pronounced perfect and Ray planned that her crew was to consist only of the new pilot, Gary, and himself. But he had reckoned without Lola.

The plan of attack was simplicity itself. At Gary's command, the thirty vessels were to take off from their several locations and were to gather en masse at twenty thousand feet altitude over the city of Philadelphia, which was about central with reference to the various flying fields. From this point the voyage to the other side of the moon was to commence, the *Meteor* leading with five of the new vessels, two of which were to have the G-ray armament. The remaining twenty-five were to follow in groups of five, each group including two of the ships with G-ray generators. Upon reaching their destination an immediate assault on the enemy was to be made and no cessation of hostilities was to be permitted until the entire enemy fleet and the lunar base was destroyed. The fleet was next to proceed to Callisto and engage the fifty space fliers that were reported as awaiting news of the success of the first fleet.

At the hour set for the departure the *Meteor* was ready in her own enclosure. At the controls sat Marshall Bostwick and, watch in hand, Ray faced the microphone through which his orders were to be issued. Gary was engaged in clamping the outer door of the air lock.

"Attention, squadron commanders," spoke Ray. "All ready?"

There followed the assenting replies from the commanders of the five squadrons and from the temporary commander of his own group. Then came the order to take off and, as the *Meteor* taxied across its field and roared over the treetops, they knew that the other thirty vessels of the fleet were likewise taking to the air. The *Meteor* climbed rapidly to twenty thousand feet and headed southward.

With all their attention focused on the instrument board and the controls, the three men were astonished beyond measure at the silvery tinkle of feminine laughter that assailed their ears. Ray swung about as if on a pivot.

"Lola!" he gasped.

"Yes, it is Lola." The girl had crept from her hiding place amongst the blankets in one of the bunks. "You did not think that this so grand war could be fought without Lola, did you?"

"Why—why," Ray stammered. Then he was forced to laugh in spite of himself. "But I guess it's all right," he concluded lamely.

"Most certainly it is all right, Ray. Lola must be with you when you free her own country. Is it not true?"

"Yes it is true, my dear," he admitted readily, "and I am very sorry that I did not see it in that light before. You are welcome aboard the *Meteor*.

"Lola is glad," she stated simply.

And Ray and Gary were glad too, but Marshall Bostwick was not so sure. He was a matter-of-fact sort of chap and the idea of having a woman mixed up in this mess did not appeal to him. But then, he had not known Lola previously.

They were soon at the appointed meeting place and within a very few minutes the entire fleet had assembled, the key squadron of five of the larger ships taking its place behind the *Meteor*. Without further delay Ray's orders were forthcoming and the fleet headed skyward with gradual acceleration to the velocity required in escaping the gravity attraction of the Earth.

One by one the vessels of the fleet reported that all portions of their apparatus were functioning perfectly and by this time a speed of two thousand miles a minute had been reached. Ray drew a breath of relief and ordered all ships to maintain this rate of speed. They would arrive at their destination, the moon, in about two hours.

As the Earth receded rapidly astern and the moon's disc evolved into a clearly defined globe of ever-increasing size and brilliancy, Marshall Bostwick could not restrain his exclamations of surprise and wonder. Ray and Gary exchanged smiles over the thought of how many expressions of similar wonder must at this moment be vented on board the other thirty vessels, none of whose occupants had ever seen the marvels of the universe under such conditions. The moon rushed toward them with terrifying rapidity and the great flaming orb of the sun seemed stationary in the blackness of the firmament, its most brilliant prominences partly hidden behind Earth, which was now presented as a crescent with fully three quarters of the visible surface in semidarkness.

The trip was uneventful and of unbelievably short duration. As they approached the brilliant near side of the satellite, Ray issued his orders and the fleet swung about to encircle the body at about three thousand miles distance. The speed was reduced gradually until they were traveling at no more than a tenth of the previous rate. At the reduced speed they drew closer to the surface and in about twenty minutes had reached the point where a sharply defined shadow told of the merging of the daylight of the moon into its long night. They crossed into the darkness of the other side and were headed toward the huge sea at whose precipitous shore the Callistonian village was located and at which point they expected to find the enemy fleet.

The first engagement of the war was about to begin.

CHAPTER SEVENTEEN
A Surprise Attack

WITH the sun no longer visible, the blackness of the heavens became still deeper and the stars shone with magnificent splendor. At the horizon the great gleaming crescent of the Earth sank from view with majestic grandeur. Venus shone brilliantly in the sky and the reddish point of light that was Mars took on an importance and beauty it had never presented before. The darkness on the surface was not complete, for the combined light from the naked stars provided sufficient visibility, so that the great craters and their central spires could be made out dimly when the eyes of the observers became accustomed to the comparative obscurity. But it was necessary that the automatic heating apparatus of the vessels come into operation to keep their interiors at normal temperature in the moon's shadow.

When they had proceeded another quarter of the way around the satellite, Ray called for a halt and for a drop to within two or three miles of the surface. With this accomplished, he searched the dim-lit landscape below with powerful night glasses and soon made out the locality of the village and the fleet of the enemy. As they drew nearer, all observers were able to make out the shapes of the fifty Callistonian vessels, for numerous round windows in the vessels were illuminated by lights from within. The village too showed lights, so there was no difficulty in reaching close range for a surprise attack. Three of the squadrons were directed to spread out and encircle the area including the village and the open space where the huge enemy vessels reposed. These were to watch for surprise counterattacks by the Callistonians and were to utilize fusing beam and G-ray generators where necessary, as well as the paralyzing energy, in cases where any of the enemy might venture forth in their airtight suits. The *Meteor* and the other half of the fleet were to make the main attack, relying principally on the G-rays and the suddenness of their onslaught.

All lights on the Tellurian vessels had been extinguished and Ray gave orders that the searchlights were not to be used, unless it became absolutely necessary, when they were to be directed at the individual warships of the enemy to serve the double purpose of illuminating the hulls and of blinding the enemy observers. When the squadron commanders reported that fifteen Tellurian ships now encircled the foe, the order to attack was given.

"Marsh" said Ray to his pilot, "keep your eyes peeled now and your fingers on the rocket controls. I am going to handle the G-ray and Gary will use the fusing beam. All set now."

The last was spoken into the microphone and simultaneously with the words the *Meteor* swooped directly for the center of the huddled mass of spheres, followed in this maneuver by the fifteen vessels of their own fleet. Seven faintly visible purplish rays impinged upon seven of the great spheres and nine of the fusing beams searched for vulnerable spots in the hulls of the enemy ships.

"Holy Smoke!" shouted Gary. "Just look at that!"

He was watching the sphere at which Ray had directed his G-ray. It had flattened itself to a crushed mass of twisted metal and one of the nearby vessels crashed into the wreckage with such force as to split itself asunder and spew forth its machinery and occupants into the deep powder that carpeted the surface. To the left there shot forth from another of the spheres a blast of incandescent particles that resembled the discharge of a Bessemer converter. A fusing beam had contacted with the upper protuberance of this ship and the escaping air from the interior carried away the white hot metal in a shower of sparks that lighted the scene brilliantly. The attackers withdrew momentarily to observe the result of the first onslaught.

Fully ten of the huge spheres were crushed by their tremendous increase in weight caused by the action of the G-rays. Five more were flaming torches from successful operation of the fusing beams. But the remainder of the fleet had come to life and several of the vessels had already left their positions and were rising to the defense. From these there came the beams of searchlights that hunted the skies for the cause of the unexpected disaster. One of these beams lighted up the tapering hull of a Tellurian vessel and two of the yellow rays converged immediately to contact with the unwelcome visitor. Ray and Gary watched spellbound as this ship of their own fleet hovered helplessly for a moment and then plunged to the ground, entirely out of control.

Lola cried out, "Oh, what if Ed-dee is on that ship? He will be killed and it is all Lola's fault."

But she soon forgot her fear and became absorbed in the scene of action that quickly developed. The outer ring of Tellurian vessels had brought their searchlights into play and an arena of great brilliance was outlined beneath them. There was confusion in the village and confusion in the maneuvers of the spherical ships in the plain. Two of the caterpillar tractors lumbered forth from the village, their yellow rays searching the skies for the ships of the invaders. Numbers of ballooned helmeted figures could be seen rushing from the doors of the cylindrical buildings. Three of the gigantic spheres, which had risen some distance from the surface, came crashing down, welded into a solid mass of distorted metal by the terrific mutual attraction set up by one of the G-rays.

Another of the Tellurian vessels was down and the *Meteor* rose rapidly to attack a number of the spheres that had reached an advantageous position. The key squadron followed and they made short work of the Callistonians who had ventured aloft, the simultaneous action of three of the G-rays hurling five of the gigantic spheres into a death huddle that provided a vivid pyrotechnic display and a crash below, that half buried the wrecked machines in the lunar dust. Beneath them the scene was indescribable. Even the cylindrical habitations of the Callistonians had flattened into unrecognizable masses of metal under the influence of the G-rays. Not a living being was in sight, all having been either killed in the wreckage of their habitations or stretched lifeless in the dust by the action of the paralyzing energy of the Tellurians. As the *Meteor* approached the scene, one of the big spheres rose to meet the tiny vessel and the yellow ray spurted forth so suddenly that Lola screamed in alarm. But the Callistonian was too late, for already the G-ray had found its mark and the sphere rolled over on its side, thus sending the yellow ray wide of its mark. It poised for a second or two in this position and then, with inconceivable acceleration, hurtled to its destruction against the edge of the precipice.

The encircling squadrons of Ray's fleet had converged on the remaining scattered spheres and a dozen individual encounters were in progress. At one point Ray saw that three of the spheres had attacked a lone Tellurian vessel and he hurled his squadron to the assistance of the besieged ship. This was the most serious single encounter of the battle and two of Ray's squadron of five ships went crashing to destruction, one of these being caught between two of the spheres when they crashed together under the influence of the G-rays. But, with this engagement ended, there remained but six of the big spheres and these made a frantic effort to escape. At Ray's quick command, three squadrons of his fighting ships darted skyward with bright streams of burning gases from their rocket tubes marking their trail. The rest of his fleet landed amongst the ruins of the Callistonian vessels where five of the graceful ships from Earth also lay helpless in the thick dust.

Then came a triumphant report from the blackness of the heavens and Ray doffed the headphones of the radio with satisfaction.

"All six of the escaping vessels have been destroyed," he stated. "The commander of the A-7 advises that they crashed at a point some fifty miles from us. Now we'll see if any of our comrades are still alive in the ships that were brought down."

Lola was weeping as he pulled on his airtight suit and she begged for permission to accompany them on the search. Her own trappings were still aboard the *Meteor* and Ray had not the heart to refuse her request. So, when all three were fully clothed in the flexible suits and with the bulky helmets locked in place, he and Gary and the Callistonian maiden stepped from the outer door and into the scene of carnage.

Meanwhile the remainder of the fleet had landed and Ray was overjoyed to see that one of the vessels he had thought destroyed was rising from its position, apparently unharmed. The effects of the yellow ray had worn off and the commander, discovering that his apparatus was once more in order, was experimenting with a view of determining whether the ship could be navigated. But four Earth vessels lay where they had fallen and Ray's party immediately set forth to investigate their condition.

The victory had been a glorious one but Ray hated to lose even a single vessel. And Lola was hurrying with all possible speed to learn whether any of the four disabled ships were from America.

CHAPTER EIGHTEEN
By Radio with A-4

SEVERAL hours were spent in searching the wreckage of the Earth vessels, all four of which were so seriously damaged that portions of the hulls had been torn open, thus allowing the oxygen to escape from within and causing the suffocation of the crews. The bodies were all recovered and a decent burial was accorded their comrades by numbers of enlisted men from the other vessels who had joined the searching party from the *Meteor*. One of the destroyed vessels was the A-3, an American-made and American-manned ship, and when the bodies were taken from this one Lola examined each one carefully through the thick window of her oxygen helmet. But she was unable to recognize the features of Eddie Dowling among those horribly swelled and bloated corpses.

The Callistonian vessels were twisted and torn and smashed beyond belief. Those that had been brought down by the G-ray were literally smashed into the ground and had burst open from the impact, which had crushed them flat. Those with openings burned through the hulls were not otherwise badly damaged, excepting in those cases where they had dropped from a considerable height, but it was clearly impossible that any living creatures remained within them on account of the loss of oxygen through the great holes created by the fusing beams. The village itself was a wreck and the numbers of those Callistonians who had ventured forth in their oxygen helmets and airtight clothing were still helpless from the effects of the paralyzing rays of the Tellurians. These were about forty in number and were carried to the various vessels of the Tellurian fleet where they were restored to consciousness after being securely bound. Ray had no intention of countenancing wanton slaughter of these helpless beings.

When the Tellurians had returned to their ships and all was in readiness for the take-off, Ray tuned his radio transmitter to the frequency of the International Communications headquarters and was soon conversing with the operator on duty. He reported the results of the lunar battle and was extremely surprised at learning that the news broadcasts had already announced most of the story to the world.

"How in Sam Hill did you know?" asked Ray.

The operator laughed. "Why there were miles of tape rolling out of the recorder here, Mr. Parsons," he said. "The enemy kept their radio going until the last minute—until the village itself was destroyed—and our translations gave us a very good word picture of the whole thing right in the midst of the action. But a bad feature of it is that their home folks know all about it too, and will be prepared for you when you get there."

"Yes, that is true. They may even come out to meet us. But we have no alternative—we must proceed at once to Callisto and you can notify the news syndicate to that effect."

"Very well, Sir."

And, with a quick turn of the tuning dial, Ray was once more transmitting on the frequency to which all receivers of his fleet were tuned. The order to take off was given at once.

Within a very few minutes they were once more out of the moon's shadow and were headed for their destination on a carefully calculated path which was to measure close to 450 millions of miles. Steadily the speed was increased until they reached the unbelievable velocity of eighty thousand miles a minute. Earth and its tiny satellite were soon left far behind.

When they had settled down to a steady grind at this speed, Lola approached Ray timidly. "Will you not attempt to communicate with Ed-dee for Lola?" she asked.

"Why you poor kid," laughed Ray. "Of course I will. I should have thought of it long ago. As commander of the fleet I will now be able to get in touch with him."

No sooner were the words uttered than he turned once more to the microphone and requested the commander of the American vessel on which Eddie Dowling was carried as a member of the crew to report in. Lola stood expectantly at his side and soon there came the reply. For the first time Ray knew that Eddie was on the A-4.

"Get him on the radio, Thomas," he requested of the A-4's chief officer. And Lola clapped her little hands with joy as Ray awaited the voice of his erstwhile mechanic.

"Hello Chief," came the voice, "some fight back there on the moon, wasn't it?"

"Yes, but that's not the reason I called you. There is a little lady on board the *Meteor* who would like to speak with you."

"For the luva Pete, Chief, is Lola along with you?"

"She is, although I didn't know it until we were well on our way. She came as a stowaway. But here—I know you must be anxious to speak with her."

"No, no, now—wait a minute. I've been doing some thinking since I packed up and joined this outfit. I've been bughouse for even thinking about her. Why, doggone it, she's a princess in her own land, and after we get things straightened out up there, what chance do I stand with her? No Chief, she's not for me. I won't talk to her."

"But Eddie, you don't understand. She had a fit when she found you were gone and has been upset ever since. She wants you, man. Don't be a fool now—come on and talk to her."

He turned the headphones over to Lola and she spoke rapidly into the microphone, begging for forgiveness and understanding. Ray winked solemnly at Gary, but Marsh Bostwick listened in disgust.

Lola waited patiently for a reply but there was none. Eddie had left the radio of the A-4. Once more the girl spoke and Ray frowned in annoyance as he realized that Eddie was actually refusing to converse with her. There was silence for a moment and then Lola removed the phones and, without looking at the men, rushed to her bunk where she buried her head in the pillow.

"Why darn his hide!" commented Ray, under his breath. "What shall I do, Gary? Shall I have his captain command him to speak to her?"

"No, I wouldn't. He's just that stubborn he would be likely to refuse and would then be disciplined for insubordination. Let the thing straighten itself out—"

"I guess you're right. But Eddie is a fool just the same. A lot Lola will care whether she is a princess and he an ordinary mechanic. She proved herself when she came back from Washington."

"You've changed your mind about her I see," laughed Gary.

"Yes I have. She's a brick and I hate to see her unhappy."

They both cast affectionate glances in the direction of the girl's pathetic little figure, and somehow their eyes misted when they observed that it was shaken with soundless sobs.

Marsh Bostwick kept his fingers on the rocket control buttons and offered no comments.

IN less than four days by Earth time the fleet swung into the orbit of Jupiter and approached the huge planet at a distance of three million miles, decelerating gradually until a second change in direction was ordered to make the approach to Callisto. When the orb of the satellite loomed large in the field of the telescope of the *Meteor* it was seen that a great portion of the surface presented to view was covered with a dense layer of clouds. The reflected light was far from intense on account of the great distance from the sun, whose flaming orb had now become of small size and importance in the blackness of the firmament. Lola, more sedate and solemn than she had been since Ray and Gary first met her, clutched nervously at her throat when they drew near to the body that was her loved home. She had not spoken of Eddie since the attempt to communicate with him, but her two friends knew from her demeanor that she was suffering intensely, and as a consequence, they had made every effort to keep her entertained during the long voyage.

Their instruments soon registered the sensible gravity field of the satellite and it was not long until they approached so closely that the globe filled their entire field of vision. Still the dense cloud layer persisted and Ray had some doubts as to the advisability of diving through the rolling banks of billowy whiteness. The barometer showed a slight pressure of atmosphere outside the vessel and the speed of the fleet was reduced to less than a thousand miles an hour. They were in the atmosphere of Callisto.

Then came the Callistonian fleet, apparently the entire fifty vessels, and it rose through the clouds at a distance of not more than five miles from the Tellurian fleet. Evidently the enemy had learned of their approach by means of sound detectors or some similar means. The third great battle of the war was about to start.

CHAPTER NINETEEN
"Viljon, of the Anurdi"

THE spherical vessels, when they sighted the fleet from Earth, drew together in close formation and hovered expectantly. Ray did not know what to expect, for he knew they had been forewarned by the lunar radio, and would probably have formulated some definite method of attack. He therefore ordered his own fleet to spread out in open formation, each squadron keeping at a distance of at least one half mile from its nearest neighboring squadron. He then proceeded slowly in the direction of the motionless enemy fleet to get within range for the use of the G-ray.

They had not long to wait for action on the part of the enemy. When the *Meteor* was still more than a mile distant, there came a sudden barrage of the yellow rays—three from each spherical ship—and these were concentrated on his own squadron. Helplessly Marsh Bostwick pressed the rocket control buttons; unsuccessfully he attempted to start the motor in the forward compartment. The atmospheric density was now sufficient for the use of wings and propellers, but the ignition system failed to function due to the influence of the deadly yellow ray. And their vision was completely obscured by the intense darkness that fell about them like a pall. Ray shouted frantic orders into the microphone of the radio, which had likewise gone dead. The *Meteor* and its accompanying squadron drifted toward the satellite with ever-increasing speed. Then, just as the *Meteor* went into a tailspin from which all efforts of the pilot failed to recover, the impenetrable darkness melted into the brightness of an equally impenetrable mist and Ray knew that the effects of the yellow rays had worn off. Simultaneously with the passing of the darkness there came the startling roar of the motor and in a few seconds Marsh had pulled out of the spin and was heading the vessel into a steep climb. Then they were once more about the clouds in the pale light of the sun. Two miles ahead and several thousand feet above them was the Callistonian fleet, all of their yellow rays directed into a falling cloud of blackness that told of another of Ray's squadrons sent toward the surface. But two other squadrons had flanked the enemy fleet and he saw that they were close enough to use their G-rays and fusing beams. Then the remaining three vessels of his own squadron rose from the mists and joined the *Meteor,* which led them rapidly toward the unsuspecting enemy fleet. The Callistonians had at first made the error of attacking at too great an elevation, thus permitting their intended victims to recover from the effects of the yellow rays before crashing on the surface of the satellite. Yet two of Ray's squadrons were down.

With no less than six of the powerful G-rays directed into the mass of the spherical vessels there were almost immediate results. Suddenly the mass huddled still closer and then, with a crash that came like a terrific explosion, the entire fleet had merged into a solid agglomeration of twisted and crushed metals. Bodies of the blond giants were thrown from the ships as they burst under the impact, bodies that went hurtling toward the great cloudbanks and were swallowed up by the mists in their swift descent. Then, with a reeling lurch, the huge mass of crushed ships plunged downward so rapidly as to be swallowed by the same mists before the Tellurians fully realized what had occurred. Lola's hands were clenched so tightly together that her knuckles showed white between fingers that pressed deeply into the flesh. But her face shone with gladness, for she knew that her own people were to be forever freed from the oppression of the blond giants.

Ray issued orders with rapidity as the radiophone was restored to normal functioning, and the remnants of the fleet drew into formation and prepared for the dive through the clouds. He checked up at once and learned that six of his ships did not respond to his calls and among these six was the A-4. His heart sank when he discovered this but he did not tell Lola. Then they were in the clouds and he watched the periscope intently as Marsh maneuvered the tiny vessel to lower altitudes. He was not entirely certain of the accuracy of his altimeter on account of the peculiar gravity field of the satellite, which seemed to increase very rapidly in its effect, as they drew near its surface.

After what seemed like an endless glide, the *Meteor* emerged from beneath the clouds. It was fortunate they had proceeded so cautiously for the "ceiling" was no more than fifteen hundred feet above the surface. The fleet was directly over a city of considerable size, which was surrounded by a broad wall of glistening metal. And a huge corner of this city lay a pulverized mass of ruins where the pile of Callistonian vessels had landed and half buried itself in the surface, carrying buildings, wall, and living beings with it.

"Viljon!" exclaimed Lola, "the capital city of the Anurdi, the enemies of my own people. This is their great stronghold and much care must now be taken."

But the city was a bedlam of excitement and the inhabitants could be observed milling around in the narrow streets, apparently in a frenzy of fear. The buildings were not of the cylindrical type that had been erected by the Anurdi on the moon, but they seemed to be of the same kind of metal. It was a city of not more than five stories in height, with all buildings of monotonous similarity in size and shape. Each building filled a complete block between the narrow thoroughfares, which were laid out in absolute parallelism. At a number of points along the remaining sections of the wall there were towers, and Ray suspected that these were provided with penetrators of the yellow ray and possibly with the attracting force of the Anurdi as well. He therefore directed his vessels to concentrate the combined energy of their G-rays and fusing beams on these points. The results were immediate and complete, for each tower crumpled into a mass `of crushed and semi-molten metal under the onslaught. The frenzy of the inhabitants increased to the proportions of an uncontrollable uprising. Then, in an open space in the center of the city, a mob of citizens could be seen unfurling a large banner of snowy whiteness. The Anurdi were suing for peace!

Ordering the remainder of his fleet to hover over the city, Ray directed his own pilot to land the *Meteor* in the open square where the white flag was displayed. As they descended it was observed that many small aircraft were on top of the flat-roofed buildings but that none were in the air. It was evident that the Anurdi were thoroughly cowed by the Tellurian armada. And indeed this was no wonder, for the flower of their young manhood had been wiped out of existence with the annihilation of their fleet by the Tellurians.

Lola was recognized by Ja-tal, ruler of the Anurdi, a giant among giants. It was he who greeted the little party from the *Meteor* when it landed and, scorning a bodyguard, made overtures for peace with Lola as interpreter. The treaty of Viljon, later signed, was based on these preliminary negotiations and its provisions are now so well known as to make it unnecessary to go into them in any detail. Of prime importance to Lola was the agreement that all Anurdi forces withdraw from Dassan, her own native land. But to the Tellurians the assurance of lasting peace between Tora and Thares came as a complete triumph, and the garrisons of Earth, that later became permanent landmarks throughout Anurdi, did not lack for volunteers from all nations.

With the preliminary negotiations completed and the city of Viljon changed from a chaos of fear to a scene of jubilant celebration, the *Meteor* once more took to the air, and headed the search for the vessels that had been brought down by the yellow rays of the Anurdi. All of these were found outside the city walls and the first three that were located were seen to be complete wrecks with all occupants either killed or dying.

Then they came to the A-4 and Lola's hands again fluttered to her throat, as they observed that the ship was scarcely damaged and that a number of its crew were busily engaged about the landing gear, endeavoring to restore the partly overturned vessel to an even keel. The other two ships of the Earth fleet were close by, and these too seemed to be but slightly damaged and with full crews clustered about them. The Tellurians had lost but three of their vessels.

Overjoyed, Lola was first to step from the *Meteor* when it landed beside the A-4 and she rushed to where Eddie, in grimy overalls and with a huge wrench in his hands, was at work on one of the landing gear struts.

"Ed-dee," she addressed him timidly.

A broad black smear appeared on his forehead as he drew his hand across it in surprise. "Why, hello, Lola," he returned lamely.

Just then, with a roaring swoop, there landed a Callistonian-airplane, a craft very similar to those in use on Earth. It was a ship from Dassan, and when it landed a group of Lola's own people rushed to the A-4 and surrounded her before she could converse further with the much-flustered mechanic. Protesting vainly, she was swept from Eddie's side.

Then a handsome youth of Dassan, garbed in a magnificent purple costume of the skin-tight variety worn by all of his people, swept her into his arms and literally carried her into the newly arrived plane. Eddie gazed after them with openmouthed astonishment and with a sinking heart. Lola already had a lover, and of her own kind!

CHAPTER TWENTY
Eddie Returns to the Meteor

TWO of the Dassanese were left behind when their plane took off, one to accompany the *Meteor* and to direct its pilot in leading the main body of the Tellurian fleet to Sharan, the capital of Dassan, the other to remain with the three slightly damaged Tellurian ships and to direct them to the same location when repairs were completed. By arrangement with the commander of the A-4, Ray exchanged Marsh Bostwick for the disconsolate Eddie, whom he returned to the *Meteor* as its pilot.

"Hello Eddie," Gary greeted him, when they were about to board the *Meteor*, "why so pensive?"

"Oh now, lay off the kidding," replied Dowling. "You know what is wrong with me. I'm a nut too for taking it this way, but I want no wise cracks about it."

"No offense, old man," said Gary. "And I want to tell you that you are all wrong about Lola too. Don't give up so easily."

"I know when I am licked, Gary. Didn't you see the guy who carried her into the plane? Swell chance I've got."

"That may not mean a thing. He may be a cousin or something. At any rate, Lola's actions during the trip showed us what she thinks of you. Stick to it, and I'll bet you get her, Eddie."

"Cousin, my eye. You never saw any cousins as affectionate as those two were. Anyhow, I don't want to talk about it anymore."

So Gary desisted and Eddie took the pilot's seat as Ray entered the cabin with Thard, the Dassanese navigator. Thard was a well-set man of medium height and had a pleasant and friendly manner. Of course he could speak no word of English, so it had been arranged that he would direct the Tellurian fleet by means of plotting the course on a chart of Thares, with which he had been provided. The Dassanese plane had taken off and had long since vanished in the distance, when Ray issued orders for the fleet to take to the air.

It was with keen interest that the occupants of the *Meteor* examined the chart that Thard spread before them. From it they saw that Callisto was mostly covered by water and that, with the exception of a few small islands, there were but two continents. These were Dassan and Anurdi, and Thard pointed out that Viljon, which they were just leaving, was close to the seacoast.

So it was, that they soon headed over the great sea of Pasara, as it was designated by Thard, with the fleet stringing along behind its tiny flagship. The journey was one of about three thousand miles, as nearly as Ray could estimate from the supposed diameter of Callisto, so he set the speed at five hundred miles an hour in order to reach their destination in six hours.

The ocean, strangely, showed a muddy red-brown, instead of the deep greenish-blue of the oceans on Earth. Of course the weather was extremely cloudy and that had some effect on the apparent color of the water, but he and Gary decided that it was mainly due to a high concentration of certain minerals in solution or in suspension, possibly iron oxides. The surface was troubled and choppy, though there was very little wind, but Thard did not seem to be concerned about the weather so the Tellurians presumed that conditions were more or less normal for the world they were visiting.

Ray made some tests of the outside atmosphere and found that it was of nearly the same density and composition as that of the Earth. However he found certain peculiarities in the gravity of Callisto, which could only be accounted for on the assumption that there was a gravity force separate and distinct from that due to the mass of the body alone. The altimeter depended on normal Earth gravity and, while the surface gravity of Thares appeared to be about the same as that of Tora, its indications became widely erroneous when at any considerable altitude. The force did not vary inversely as the square of the distance from the body, but at a much higher rate, thus confirming Ray's previous supposition, that there was a supplementary force that accounted for the high surface gravity of so small a body and its retention of so considerable an atmosphere. This they learned later was due to an extremely high percentage of magnetic ores in the interior of the body; the peculiar properties of whose magnetic fields were quite similar to the artificial gravity set up by the G-rays.

When they approached the shores of Dassan the skies were clearing, and soon the sun shone forth weakly, as if it were some infinitely remote body, that seemed scarcely akin to the sun that shone on Earth. But the temperature of the air was nearly eighty degrees, and the two scientists from Tora were forced to the conclusion that it was warmed by the internal heat of the satellite. They later learned that the assumption was nearly correct, although the warm climate of Thares was actually brought about by the presence of huge deposits of radioactive minerals near the surface, rather than by the high temperature of a molten interior. The waters brightened somewhat with the coming of the noonday sun, though they still retained the red-brown color to a great degree. The sun itself was almost at the zenith, thus indicating that about half of the long Callistonian day had passed—half of a day, which in Earth time was the equivalent of more than sixteen and a half days. Darkness would not come for a long time.

Thard was busy with the charts but he looked up with a pleased smile at the delighted exclamations that came from the visitors at their first view of the land of Dassan. The *Meteor* was speeding inland and the landscape below was of infinite variety and great beauty. They were over a rolling countryside, which gave every evidence of the bounties of nature and the handiwork of a highly intelligent and industrious people. Uncultivated portions were lush with brilliant vegetation-hues and tints there were that would have delighted an artist. Farmlands showed great fields of perfect symmetry and with fully developed crops of strange grains and vegetables—strange for their color as viewed from the air. Purples and browns were the predominating hues and the Earth visitors had no means of knowing whether these were the colors of ripe or unripe crops. But it was a beautiful and interesting country and the occasional towns and villages over which they passed proved equally interesting and inviting.

Now they were over a city of considerable size and it was seen that much more of artistic ability had been expended in its planning than was the case in Viljon. These people did not adhere to the mathematical precision of their enemies in laying out the streets. Here there were many beautiful parks, circular in shape and with broad radiating streets that curved and wound in all directions through attractive residence districts where no two dwellings were of the same size or architectural design. Then they were once more in the open country, and the cloud of small aircraft that had surrounded them when they passed over the city, drifted away and the individual planes returned to their normal activities. The welcome accorded the fleet by such craft was a feature of the journey inland that marked the approach to each city of any size near which they passed, and it was extremely gratifying to the Tellurians.

When eventually they reached Sharan they found it the largest and most beautiful city of all, and its streets were bright with gay banners and buntings. They were welcomed in the air by six planes that flew in formation with the dignity of an official flight. By their maneuvers the six planes indicated that the Tellurian fleet was to follow in their wake, and when this was done, they soon reached a great amphitheater where thousands of the Dassanese had assembled, and where a huge landing space had been roped off in the center of the field. Lightly the *Meteor* dropped to a landing, the larger vessels following closely behind.

Upon the disembarkment of the Earth visitors from their ships, a great hubbub of cheering came up from the assembled multitude and a group of gaily-adorned Dassanese approached the four men who stood at the door of the *Meteor.* Among these was Lola and she was at the side of the handsome youth who had greeted her so enthusiastically outside of Viljon. In fact they were holding hands when they drew near the *Meteor's* party and their faces were alight with happiness.

"See?" whispered Eddie. "What did I tell you? Fat chance there is for the little fat mechanic!"

"Oh, hush up!" hissed Ray, for the group was now very close by.

CHAPTER TWENTY-ONE
A Happy Ending

AT each Tellurian vessel, its crew stood at attention, the men dazzled by the magnificence of the amphitheater and confused by the shouting of the crowds. Lola's party, with Ray at the girl's side and Gary and Eddie bringing up the rear, visited every vessel of the fleet, and at her request, the crews were ordered to proceed to the great dais, which was seen in the field that faced the crowded tiers of seats. When the Tellurians had assembled and marched toward the dais in splendid military form, the demonstrations of the crowd came to a climax of tremendous enthusiasm. And when the three Earthmen from the *Meteor* were seen to accompany her to the seats of honor on the platform, the entire assemblage rose to stand in grateful recognition. With her guests all seated close by, Lola mounted the steps of a secondary platform on which were two gorgeously upholstered seats over which appeared a fan-shaped, jeweled emblem that was evidently the insignia of royalty in this strange land. She was not alone, for the handsome youth in purple followed her and faced with her a battery of what were obviously the microphones of a public address system.

The huge assemblage became still as Lola raised her hand and started speaking in her own tongue. She was radiantly flushed and was once more attired in a silver costume such as she had worn when the Earthmen first took her into the *Meteor* on the other side of the moon. So beautiful she seemed when she raised her sweet voice in addressing her people that Eddie whispered an "ah" of admiration. But this changed to a muffled growl of annoyance when he saw that the handsome youth at her side had once more captured her hand and now held it tightly as if in the assurance of possession.

Lola's speech was of considerable length and was delivered with great vigor. The Dassanese listened to her in deferential silence for the space of many minutes. Then she turned in Ray's direction and addressed him in his own tongue.

"If it please you, my dear Ray," she said, "kindly step to the platform at my side."

Somewhat flustered at the request, he acceded, and the ensuing roar from the multitude served only to increase his embarrassment. Then Lola raised her hand once more and the crowd became silent as she renewed her speech. From the few words he was able to catch and from her continued repetition of his name he knew she was telling of his part in the salvation of Dassan.

At the conclusion of this address and the renewal of the cheering, Ray bowed and returned to his own seat.

"Glad that's over," he whispered to his companions, wiping great beads of perspiration from his brow.

Then a group of three men of Dassan mounted the small platform and faced Lola and her male companion. These were older men and were attired in long robes of red that trailed the platform as they walked. The one in advance of the other two carried a golden scepter in his hand and with this he touched Lola's forehead, the while he read in a steady monotone from a small volume he held in his other hand. A deathly silence reigned throughout the amphitheater and Eddie drew in his breath quickly as the significance of this ceremony became evident to him. Priests, these robed Dassanese were, and they were performing a marriage ceremony! Lola was forever lost to him!

The rite was simple but impressive and Gary and Ray assiduously refrained from looking in Eddie's direction, knowing that his feelings would be pictured tragically on the chubby countenance. Now the priest had touched the forehead of the handsome youth with scepter, his voice still droned monotonously as he read from the ritual. Then it was over. The youth kissed Lola on the forehead and bedlam once more broke loose in the stands. Many of the nobles of Dassan crowded to the couple on the small platform, evidently to express their congratulations.

Not until then did Ray steal a glance at Eddie, and he was genuinely concerned at the sickly pallor that had spread over his friend's features.

"Eddie old man," he admonished him, "don't you care. It's tough luck I know, but don't let it get your goat."

Then a surprising thing happened for Lola struggled from the midst of the group on the platform and rushed to where the crew of the *Meteor* sat. The nobles still remained with the handsome youth she had left behind and showered him with adulation.

"Ray; Gair-ree; Ed-dee," panted the excited Lola. "Listen to Lola while she explains what has transpired. I told my people of the so great bravery of you three in rescuing Lola from the persecution of La-dar on the satellite of Tora. I told them of the kindness of your people to Lola when she was on Tora. I told them of all that has happened since, and of Ray's leadership of the so successful expedition to Thares. My people are now free—the Anurdi have surrendered their weapons and their positions of authority and are leaving Dassan. All is to be happiness once more. And to Lola comes the greatest happiness of all."

Eddie hung on her words, his heart in his eyes.

"Yes," she continued, "for Lola there is the greatest joy of all. Lola's people begged her to take the throne of her parents, since to her it belongs by right of succession. But Lola refused and only now has the scepter been transferred to Lola's younger brother. Only now is that brother, Boruth, accepting the felicitations of the members of his court. Lola is free to choose her mate."

"Ye gods!" gasped Eddie. "Her brother! Well—I'll be hornswaggled!"

Lola was advancing directly to the suddenly flushed and smiling mechanic. She held out her arms and Ray and Gary turned quickly away, their eyes once more misty.

* * *

FIVE years have passed since the war with Callisto and times have greatly changed. The devastated areas in the great cities of Earth have been completely rebuilt and are in every respect much improved by the rehabilitation. The scars left by the raid of the Anurdi have mostly healed.

Larger replicas of the vessels designed by Ray Parsons have made possible the establishment of regular traffic between Callisto and the Earth. Great liners now make the journey in less than three days and much benefit has accrued to the inhabitants of both bodies. The Anurdi have accepted their lot stoically, and some say, have actually welcomed the change. Tellurians who man the many forts that were erected throughout Anurdi report that no troubles of any kind have been experienced and that conditions in all parts of the country are excellent. In Dassan there have settled many adventurers from all parts of the Earth and these are in the habit of visiting their former homes occasionally and boasting of the many advantages of living on Thares. Conversely, there are hundreds of Dassanese now on Earth and these are equally enthusiastic over their change in residence. Many people, like certain flowers, seem to thrive best when transplanted.

The radio used by the Anurdi in communicating with their lunar base was destroyed, so Gary Walton has perfected a most powerful apparatus of his own and is now installing a station in Sharan, by means of which it is hoped that reliable communication with Earth may be effected.

Ray Parsons is even more deeply immersed in his scientific work than before. After refusing all rewards offered him by the nations of the world, he set about exploring distant bodies of the solar system. Finding Mars and Venus hostile and undesirable fields for investigation, he determined to search further. Jupiter and Saturn were both visited and found uninhabitable, but he discovered a highly developed form of life inhabiting Titan, one of Saturn's moons. He spent more than a year on this satellite and returned with much valuable knowledge. His next venture will include visits to Uranus and Neptune. What may come of this great jump into space can but be conjectured.

Eddie still works in the Parsons laboratories, but has been promoted to the position of chief assistant and has complete charge in the absence of Ray. Eddie has lost much of his rotundity but is still the smiling-faced chap of the old days. And, not many miles from the laboratory, there is the modest dwelling that is home to him now—the happiest home in the universe, Lola claims.

THE END

www.ingramcontent.com/pod-product-compliance
Lightning Source LLC
Chambersburg PA
CBHW050043180626
46810CB00002B/867